PRAI

"I'm awestruck by Joe Koch's nonstop spellbinding, almost paralyzingly inventive and yet propulsive, ultra-focused prose. *The Wingspan of Severed Hands* is a truly amazing find."

— DENNIS COOPER (*THE MARBLED SWARM, THE SLUTS*)

"Koch's latest novella is what might have happened if Robert W. Chambers had been a surrealist with a penchant for body horror. A strange trip to Carcosa offered in thickly evocative language, *The Wingspan of Severed Hands* is a highly original hallucination."

— BRIAN EVENSON (*SONG FOR THE UNRAVELING OF THE WORLD, A COLLAPSE OF HORSES*)

"Joe Koch is a stunning and talented writer, and their new book, *The Wingspan of Severed Hands,* is a horror story that opens new vistas in the genre."

— JACK ZIPES (*LITERATURE AND LITERARY THEORY: FAIRY TALES AND THE ART OF SUBVERSION*)

THE WINGSPAN OF SEVERED HANDS

JOE KOCH

Second Edition

WP-0009

Print ISBN 9781951658069

Cover art/design by Don Noble

Editing and internal layout/formatting by Sam Richard

Weirdpunk Books logos by Ira Rat

Weirdpunk Books

www.weirdpunkbooks.com

Joe, thanks for the dare.
Jen, thanks for the lake.

CONTENTS

I. EGG: EUTHANASIA DAYS

Flowers in her hair, flowers in her eyes, flowers in her mouth, each step down the aisle tripped wires on a spiral-spring trap. Forced to fit into her mother's dress, her mother's mother's dress, the heirloom lace snared Adira's struggling flesh like a hunter's net. The dress, the dress, nothing like the girl, cleaned and made right for this special day. Adira's unruly body refused discipline, an animal intent on its desires, offending the ceremony, defiling the dress. No choice after her mother caught them, not their fearful fleeing bodies, not the boy in the act of wheedling, but their stripped and scattered clothes abandoned in the den. Hateful alarm, the door-knob clicked.

Animal panic. Adira's mother came home early.

Split apart naked, two bodies on opposite axes severed the single-wide home. The den, kitchenette, and living room condensed in one clean cage. The boy flew out the window, more bulk than bird, crushing crickets and twisting an ankle with his tumble. It was spring, a hot night, no screen, no darkness to blanket the bawdy scene. Adira went off to her room like a gunshot; door slammed and locked, wedding bells ringing in her ears like the aftermath of a rifle blast. No escape. She'd said no twenty-three times (she counted) until the boy turned broody and she gave in.

Now shaking, naked, pressed against the door of her room as if her wrong body reinforced its battlements with incorrect strength, blood smeared on wood, blood from her thigh, not as much as she'd expected, not much at all considering the stab. Between her legs and in the void masked by bone, her pelvic crown circled an empty universe where pain hatched. Listening: footsteps, path to the window, path to the door; an exhausted sigh. Moments of silence, aching with fear. Her mother's heavy tread down the folding metal stairs. Footsteps crunching in gravel out back. Voices without words, first low and conspiratorial, then appeasing and polite.

Adira's impolite body incapable of right form, right movement. The right action was to grab the tell-tale garments from the den. Frozen in fear of exposure, prey snared: Adira braced against a contractual laugh. Footsteps at her door, the only barrier against threats, slaps.

Her mother's phlegmatic voice broke through. "Do you want your clothes back or should I put them in the wash?"

Question like a cage, like a cancer, every answer a transfer of guilt.

Adira whispered, "Wash."

"I can't hear you, honey. You need to learn to speak up."

Couldn't speak with the web of fear spinning from her gut. Adira's inertia bound her, a wounded spider, a sacrificial cocoon cannibalized by mothers and mates. Her full flesh too unctuous not to taste, as if her succulent meat ripened only for others, bred to be devoured, stock fed and farmed for slaughter.

Adira's mother offered an incantation of obedience. Dysfunctional deception, so simple to don, a thick wet cloak inviting Adira to pull it shuddering over her eyes. "It's for your own good, honey. You know how much I love you."

Rising expectations as her mother waited for Adira's reply. Rites of acceptance, domestic mergers of identity under the title of love, love so strong it looked like hate. *I love you,* the canonical phrase, enforced daily, hourly, as often as needed to mask her mother's hungry, fleshless face. Intoned *ad nauseam,* an emetic repetition, a bulimic response, a slick tentacle gagging Adira's throat to bring up her mother's semi-digested feast. The answer voided agency from Adira's mouth, voided meaning from the words.

The phrase once spoken must be spoken back.

Defying the law of call and response, Adira left a vacancy hanging in the air. Through the closed door, the thin membrane of her penetrable fortress, a tentacle untethered as Adira gloated over the hesitation of shock. Silence followed the march of her mother's wounded retreat.

By morning, Adira's mother vomited in bed with a migraine, curtains closed against daylight. Adira cloistered and cursed her bladder's betrayal, desperate to reach the small mobile home's one bathroom through the sick dragon's lair. Her mother feigned weakness beneath blanketed dunes. Adira knew the dragon had the power to strike with the poison tentacles of its forked tongue. Fueled by fury, gorgon of the hungry eyes, the snake-haired dragon aimed at Adira, ever ready to bite.

Snuffing out the sound of her steps, Adira made the delicate journey as the dragon slept. Relief was an echoing waterfall, cascading too loud in the humid cube. Trapped and frozen anew in pink-tiled quandary, Adira listened for the groan of bedsprings, the slippery shuffle of covers, or the sigh of the fire-breathing beast.

Captive in the dragon's cave, sweat sent Adira into shivers. The walls tightened against her shoulders. She counted by fives to settle her mind. Five, ten, fifteen, twenty. The shower stall was damp, always damp. Sickening snails of moisture snaked down the tempered glass. Scummy spirals and sinister lesions hung sticky with wiggling beads. Adira trembled with a droplet that bulged like a great bulbous eye and popped from its socket. It stared with salacious horror and an alien's incomprehensible lust while the walls of the small room sweated and shook. Naked, the eye leaned forward and dangled on a wet optic nerve rooted to the glass. It swelled in obscene colors like swirling oil as it ogled Adira on the toilet.

What peered from the void beyond the Hyades dwelled in the ancient memory of the corporeal atoms of water: in her mother's angry tears, in Adira's uncontrollable sweat, in the pink dampness of the dragon's cave. Awash in endless shame, her mother's house a maze of endless traps and endless eyes, Adira sensed something distant hunted between her legs.

She jolted up. Too fast, pain from groin to heel, piss and blood leaking hot with fear. An unseen hand opened inside her vagina and bloomed red. Eyes of moisture tickled like fingertips, traced obscenities in the humid warmth clinging to her thigh.

In the open medicine chest door, the back of the mirror cancelled Adira's image in its matte grey surface. She donned the smooth silvered mask as she put on a clean pad. She zipped with disciplined calm, counted by sevens, calm, calmer, calmest, and almost made it past the bedroom in the clear. Forty-nine, fifty-six, sixty-three, seventy, seventy-seven, eighty.

The dragon reared before her exit, emaciated and expectant. Her mother's accusing eyes were as black as twin dead suns sinking into a motionless lake. "Young lady, I have one question for you." Adira froze, caught in the gorgon-like glare. Her mother asked, "Was he the first?"

Question like a cage, like a cancer, like a cudgel to the gut. A conundrum constructed to cut. Adira, on fire inside, silent.

"I think you'd better answer me, young lady."

Outside, a blubbering fountain of foolish, failed flesh. "But you...I didn't...I don't..."

Her mother, loudly: "Yes or no?"

Cold rage in her eyes, raging with jealous need and grief, holding Adira captive too long, pulling her too close in the same way she'd pulled the child Adira too often to her breast. After she miscarried her second daughter, she smothered Adira's body in a shared bed, bathed her with shame, touched her for comfort too much, too long. Fondling under the banner of love, lukewarm water went milky with disintegrating soap. Adira sucked on a washcloth to hide her resistance to the despised attention when she cried. She gagged on the scented sludge, ate the flowery taste of enforced denial. Soft as a sponge, Adira didn't say stop until she turned eight.

Wrathful wounded gorgon eyes stalked Adira's steps ever since. She'd swallowed enough stones to metabolize a mythical defense, but she saw no way to answer the question honestly without formulating it as an accusation. The aging dragon was brittle, a pale skeleton propped up by thin arms on the sickbed's yellow sheets.

Adira spoke to the floor, accepting the burden of sickness into her body, bringing the dragon back to life. "Yes."

The skeleton woman closed her eyes and leaned back in relief; the dragon breathed. "I'll get your grandmother's dress cleaned and pressed. The boy already agreed. Don't worry, honey, we'll make it right in the eyes of God."

Adira wasn't made right. Never would be. She took the dress.

THE DRESS, the dress, more precious than the thing inside. Adira packed the full bloom of her Renaissance flesh into the dress. The women on her mother's side were angular and raw, dragons sleek from internal fire that seared the excess weight off of smoldering bones. The dress fit her mother, and her mother's mother before her. If Adira's sister had been born alive, she'd have fit the dress.

"You're built like a brick house." Her mother tugged the zipper, strained the seams, and risked an explosion of Adira's lavish flesh. There was always too much of Adira. She needed to be less.

Stuffed like a butterfly forced back in its egg sac, wings amputated, antennae plucked, Adira pondered what other parts must be cut. She forced her breath out and sucked in her gut as her mother prodded her into place. "If your sister were here, everything would be different."

Adira flushed too richly, too elegantly, with too much juice as summer's soft storm turned to evening thunder and she hid her face in her refrigerated bouquet. Flowers in her hair, flowers in her eyes, flowers in her mouth. Sick rosewater vinegar fragrance of petals stuffed against her tongue. Warm thick petals, flesh flowers blooming, labia sucking her inside the mirror's gaze. She shrank from her reflection, chewing on chilled hydrangea sprays.

"Stop that. You'll ruin your makeup." Her mother shook her head, working on the fine closures that ran up the back of the bodice. The dress was an antique, designed for dainty women of another era. "You were never an easy child. Never. I tried to give you a sister, but how could I go on bed rest? I had to put food on the table. I did my best. Turn around. Let's see."

Hands all over Adira, on her hips, stomach, bust; poking, pushing, displeased.

"Let me do it." Adira turned too fast and broke a clasp.

Her mother's wounded eyes turned black.

Black as unseen fires, black as bursting suns. Black as gorgon, eyes like wounds that burned Adira's body more than the sudden slap that stung her face.

Her mother's hand still shook. She turned Adira's gaping face away. "There's no time for me to sew this. Try to stand up straight. If you act like a lady for once, no one will notice the safety pin. Don't move around too much."

Shamed by the mirror, by her mother's hand, hot and damp with uncontrollable, anxious sweat, in the dress so tight it doubled every flaw, flowers in her hair, flowers in her eyes, no time to cry. The teal church carpet reddened Adira's slapped cheek. She was a ruddy sow marched to slaughter.

Endless slaughter, the aisle stretched for miles toward an unthinkable horizon. Adira forced a step. Damp shame trickled down the crammed friction created under the dress. Sticky thighs, the smell of armpits and aftershave, the distant uncle on her arm, the strange music pulsed; Adira paced forward, accused and consumed by an ocean of eyes.

Candelabra flickered in the multitude of shining eyes like a brood of baby spiders. Eyes like pearls, like strange desires, dripping with smaller eyes that stuck to Adira's gown. Baubles from slimy depths rolled across her timid skin. Translucent turtle eggs hatched in her sumptuous fat. Eggs awakened within her. Eyes opened inside. A strange vision grew and birthed in every orifice, filled her empty cavities, gaped from within her into the distant vacuum of space.

The eyes swelled like eggs and slipped out, ready to pop. A parade of eyes rolled with lascivious moisture, melted from Adira in the spring deluge, warmed her pelvic floor, filled her belly, and burst from her vagina. Red menstrual flowers bloomed. The meat-stench of slaughter spread down the white heirloom skirt.

Arm abandoned, sanctuary aghast, Adira's unexpected blood defiled the dress. Her mother pushed through, wrapped Adira's waist with a choir robe, sleeves cinched in a bow at the back.

"Walk."

Head hung behind the bouquet, flowers forced out of season, spray of hydrangea, chewing the cud of cool petals. Flowers in her mouth, bitter velvet turned to chalk. A rose burst followed by cyanide cucumber, dry grass astringent, poison on her tongue. She bit the next petal, retched behind closed lips, chewed and swallowed again.

Down the slaughterhouse ramp, death-grip of the dragon's claw around her waist, beast bearing her body up. A camera like a sniper flashed and snapped.

"Lift your chin. You're making your face look fat."

Full of blood and poison, Adira wrenched free from her mother with a violent tug. Not her shame, not her rage, not her dress.

She dropped her arms, crushed the bouquet, and walked alone to confront the boy at the altar. Eighteen to her sixteen, oddly well-groomed in his rented tux, he cringed the closer she came. His eyes flinched with guilt. His mouth twisted, forming a defense. Adira blessed the boy with a vibrant smile. Happiness warmed her chest.

The boy looked stunned. The minister rushed.

When she kissed the groom and claimed the boy, the eyes that stared from the sanctuary didn't stick. Adira's full fertile flesh bounced them back, stuck the rotten orbs back in their glow-holes. Ribald with eyes and eggs all her own, strong and plentiful enough to populate galaxies, Adira wondered if the boy tasted the cyanide and rotten grass on her lips, and if he smelled the sumptuous space inside her that would take him over as it pressed his thigh and bled under the veil of her makeshift wrap.

THE VOMITING STARTED MID-RECEPTION. Pink petal vomit, blue acid bile, bone ivory foam. The party thumped on the restroom wall while Adira sank in her stall. Convulsions came like clockwork, hours of labor that birthed a tangible nothingness. An invisible entity emerged from Adira's empty belly, stripping unnecessary flesh from inside. Something more than biological, it lingered in the yellow pall of the spotted dance-hall mirror, crept closer in the clenched anesthetic tingling that spread on her tongue.

The angel revealed itself to Adira three hours after checking in at the hotel. Adira honeymooned alone with the toilet while the boy dozed off to porn. Emptied, Adira's gullet unburdened her. The opposite of feeding, she nurtured neither dragon nor mirror, but some innate, ineffable monster. Her body reversed, and a double formed from bloody mist. A red Hiroshima silhouette burned to life on the hotel bathroom wall.

Adira divided. Angelic cells split inside her embryonic

egg sac. Her double hatched: a nude, semi-transparent, red-tinted, skeleton girl. Shadows of bone haunted unfleshed holes within the figure's outline. Suggestions of heart and vein pulsed first in silence, then in a soft murmur as rough sketches rendered substance under elastic skin. Arteries grew with slow deliberation, red roots seeking paths in dark soil, seedlings reaching high, craving light. The skull hung down with hair long and disheveled like Adira's. Ankles crossed, toes hovering above the floor, arms bound behind her back, the twin's shoulders sprouted enormous hands that spread open like owl wings. Fingers flared like feathers with open palms forward.

Adira reached for the tips of the terrible fingers with her small, human hands, feet on tip-toes, arms spread. On contact, the double looked up. The skull sprouted flesh. Lips opened in a mute gasp. Adira flattened her breasts and belly against the double on the cool tile wall. Where she pressed her tongue, depth created a warm open mouth.

More fullness erupted where Adira made contact. Vein, sinew, and skin wrapped the bones with life. The double clutched Adira with its powerful wings. Feathers threaded fingers, whispers wedded flesh. Twin tongues circled. The tile wall melted into a red silhouette seared into liquid with menstrual excess. Liquid sought liquid. Mouths and groins spiraled. In the morphology of their melded kiss, the wings slicked with gore and lost their grip. Adira fell to the floor. The bloody twin disintegrated; a myth of angel meat, an unstable presence, a quotient reached by imbalanced belief.

The blood it left behind filled Adira with the rich, red, vibrant power of death. Red in every cell, hair thick and dripping dark; red in arms and thighs, in melted muscle and bone. Her dissipating liquid twin sloughed back into thought and left Adira alone with the blood and the boy.

One hand in his boxers, the other on his slender chest, he dozed on the hotel bed. His lips lost their sneer when he was asleep.

Adira climbed on top of the rapist and attacked with her mouth, copying his violence. The blood of twins poured onto the white hotel sheets. The boy struggled. She clamped him in her teeth. Slippery and stained, he was on top of her quickly, hands around her wrists, pinning her down. He didn't care that she was awash in blood. He said it was time to teach her a lesson. The boy pushed Adira's arms back and over her head and pressed his fingers down into her pale, putty-like flesh. Her arms squirmed like thick snakes, softer, softer. He crushed her wrists like wet clay.

He squeezed. Her arms collapsed into stumps. Her hands hit the floor like dead fish.

Not screaming, silenced by shock, Adira heard nothing after the loud, sickening slap when her amputated hands fell off. Uncertain how to breathe, she struggled to see through the crawling static that clouded her vision.

Behind the boy, wings spread. Monstrous hands opened wide, fleshy dragon wings that aimed an armory from the shoulders of a spatiotemporal anomaly. The angel-twin's mouth hung slack. It dripped with yellow bile. An egg formed like a bubble in its mouth. The boy churned his cock inside Adira with his head thrown back. The egg dropped and cracked on the boy's frontal lobe. His cranium fissured, and his spine split in half. Raw egg and boy innards slopped over Adira. Wings like hands closed over him as organs dropped out of the boy, bisected.

When police responded to calls from the neighboring rooms, the boy was gone. They found the maimed girl unconscious in gore, and a snow angel of menstrual blood smeared on the bathroom wall.

SECLUDED IN ITS SEMI-SYNTHETIC SHELL, nested in a laboratory bunker under the foothills of a distant mountain town, the embryo fed on Adira's torture dreams.

Director Bennet hid her disgust at the sight of it when she addressed the team. She'd considered their findings from an objective standpoint. She had no intention of granting Peter's request. "The aggression levels concern me."

"Aggression is the goal. We're growing a weapon, not a pet."

Bennet tapped her pen indicating where she'd made notes on his report. "Effects of this trauma aren't objectively predictable. We don't know what it's really thinking and learning in response to your input."

"That's where you're wrong. The process I employ is very much like an equation with a reliable outcome." Peter —or rather, Professor Krause, as Bennet reminded herself to call him in public—argued with typical subdued intensity. "An optimal degree of stress versus nurturance accelerates cognitive development. The trauma, as you call it, creates identification with the aggressor. It's more than neurobiology and math. We're working from holometabolous entomology, my studies in the neuroscience of mammalian dream states, and mythological models. We've linked the input to a vast literary database to inform and evolve the script."

Bennet knew the weapon was Peter's baby. She didn't question his formidable genius. She questioned his temperament. "All I can see here are bullet points. You haven't shown me any method to evaluate the results. What's happening inside the egg, other than the metabolic changes you've cited?"

"That remains to be seen. As the instars progress, we expect the subject to initiate communication."

"How will it learn to speak? Animals don't have the mouthparts to form words, in my understanding, no matter how high their intelligence."

"Insect," one of the bioengineers corrected. "The physiological form is hymenoptera. It might tap, or rub its legs and wings together to make sounds."

Bennet said, "So that's going to be subjective, and open to interpretation, am I correct?"

Peter nodded. "It's true that contact will likely be in a form we don't immediately recognize. We're prepared for that, for something equivalent to the transmission of information as it's framed in dream states."

"Like that gibberish coming out of Houston?"

No one challenged Bennet. Peter maintained his steady gaze.

While Bennet didn't mean to raise her voice in front of the whole team, she wasn't sorry that she did. Peter should be on the defensive, not her. "Recognition of symbols and sounds is ninety percent of how communication works. Without recognition on the receiving end, language is nothing but random, occult signs. You know this. We can't even debrief the recon teams anymore. All we get from them is cryptic idiocy. That is why I expect every procedure in my lab to be completely rational and transparent."

A scowl slipped across Peter's lips. "The graffiti. It's everywhere the barbarism spreads. Look, I understand you're afraid of it. You should be. People go mad when they see the image, when they even learn it exists. They carve it into their bodies, their foreheads, into the remains of their dead. Go ahead and call it by its name. Or are you afraid to say it? Why? We're all rational here. I'll say it for you. The Yellow Sign."

Everyone froze. Eyes roamed and darted around the conference table checking for a change in demeanor: a twitch, a spasm, a sign of the rumored transformative split. Bennet lamented that so many present showed by their tense response that they accepted the popular drivel about the magic sigil. Paranoid conspiracy theorists connected it to the outbreaks. Her team couldn't function efficiently if they were undermined by the terror of what they were working against.

She softened her tone. "Please, everyone, let's relax. If my esteemed colleague really believed any part of that nonsense, he'd never have spoken the words out loud. Think of the consequences implied by doing so. Please forgive him. He's having a little fun at our expense, aren't you Professor Krause?"

Their eyes met and held. Peter sat back and allowed the discomfort to fester in silence.

One of the lab techs chuckled more nervously than Bennet liked, but she was glad someone broke the spell. "Well, sure. Professor 'K' knows what he's talking about. Or else he said it out loud because he's one of those fanatics and wants to poison our brains. Guess we're all part of the cult now folks."

After a strained pause, the tech laughed again. Others joined in until Peter spoke again.

"I'm not having fun. This isn't a joke. I believe the message of the Sign is trans-conscious, and by that, I mean it is exclusively comprehensible in another dimension accessed in our dream states. This gives it intense power in our unconscious. The Sign, or whatever being or society or mechanical accident emits the Sign, operates in a state similar enough to our neurobiological dream functions to resonate with us and influence us. This resonance is strong and therefore leaves our enemy likewise susceptible to attack. That is the level my weapon will work on."

Peter turned and pointedly addressed Bennet. "And that is why we need to expand immediately and grow more weapons. The Yellow Sign is real. The madness is real. Our minds are at risk. Our souls, if you prefer the more traditional apocalyptic interpretation."

Immune to Peter's dramatics, Bennet stood and put her files in order. She took her time. "Superstitions are their own form of madness, aren't they? Setting any amateur theology aside, we'll need to understand the weapon better in order to pilot it, won't we? Hormone levels show a severe imbalance. We don't even have a baseline gyrification score yet. My veto stands firm."

Chairs and lab-coats shuffled around the conference table as the team members got up to leave. Peter remained seated. His fingers were folded together in a tighter than normal grip.

"A sample group of one subject is not a group. A sample group with no separate control is indistinguishable from a random result. If you tie my hands, this isn't a correct experiment in any sense of the word."

"Do I need to remind you how the last trial ended?"

"No, and once again, you prove my point for me. Without a sufficient sample group we have no basis for comparison. You're forcing me to proceed on a very thin body of evidence."

"Considering the confidence you expressed moments ago in your predictors, I'm a feeling bit confused." Bennet meandered closer to Peter, until she stood looking down on him. "First you said your method was as predictable as math. Now you tell me the basis for the entire profile is very thin. That's the opposite of reliable. Which is it?"

The team lingered. Peter spoke to Bennet in a subdued tone. His hand drifted towards her sleeve. "Half the Gulf Coast is already taken. It's crossed Texas into the southwest. When it heads north…you're not safe. You know how much I—"

Bennet backed away quickly. "We've got work to do. No question about that." She headed to the exit, ushering the staff out. "Great job everyone. We'll beat this thing together. What you're doing here is groundbreaking, essential work. Keep it up."

Peter sat alone at the conference table. When the last person left, Bennet closed the door and took a deep breath. She didn't turn around.

"The world's going insane," she said. "So your expert recommendation is that we overreact and risk losing everything by failing to maintain rigor and objectivity. No way. That's not how I work. We'll see how things look in the larval stage and then re-evaluate. Message me when you're ready to meet." She opened the door an inch, not quite done, poised for a fast exit. "And look, don't ever try to touch me like that in front of the staff again, for goodness sakes."

Bennet left without allowing any time for a response. She didn't expect a message from Peter anytime soon. She didn't need a statistical analysis to predict she'd likely be having dinner alone tonight. Perhaps it was for the best. Growing the experimental weapon was a sensitive project. The world was in crisis. It was depending on them. Only a flighty schoolgirl would exacerbate the tension with romantic affairs.

Maybe if we reach chrysalis without incident, Bennet thought. She rode the lift to the lower lab, enjoying the smooth sound of movement through the steel walls and the lilt in her legs when it landed. She had important decisions to make, as usual, and the brief respite in the lift was a welcome lull. *Maybe Peter and I can pick up where we left off someday. Later, when the world isn't reeling with madness, disintegrating around us like a diseased brain. Maybe we'll have a family someday, when I know there's hope for the future.*

Be strong. Bide your time.

The angel secreted a set of silver hands for Adira to wear and affixed them to her wrists. The boy was part of the angel. The angel claimed the boy and adapted his useful parts. It made slow, careful love to Adira. It learned everything about her and murmured good advice.

Killing is easy. I'll come back for you someday.

The hospital's counseling referrals outraged Adira's mother more than the maiming of her daughter, or the appearance without provenance of the elegantly wrought silver prosthetics. After a convincing performance for the social worker, Adira's mother had her discharged early and scolded her at home. "What do you mean, he's gone? Gone where? People don't vanish into thin air. What did you do?"

"I don't know. I was sick."

"I found you a husband and you let him get away, just like that? I leave you on your own for less than one week, less than one day, and you manage to lose your husband and your hands?"

He was only a boy.

"He was only a boy."

"Oh, he wasn't good enough for you, Miss High and Mighty? He was good enough to throw yourself at him under my roof and humiliate yourself. Humiliate me. I didn't raise my daughter to be a slut."

Dark, angry eyes, twin black suns sinking over lost, forbidden Carcosa. A skeleton hand reared like a banner of the king, ready to sting Adira's cheek, backside, flay her flesh to crimson strips. Lost lands and distant rivers in her mother's eyes; burning landscapes and desolate fields below broken obelisks. Nameless winds calling Adira.

I'll come back to you. Wait for me. I have to leave now.

"No. I'm leaving, too."

Her mother didn't know Adira pleaded with her invisible angel. "Honey, don't be ridiculous. You can't even feed yourself with those."

Adira's silver hands, things of beauty, works of art, made clumsy and useless by her mother's confiscating touch. Pinions oxidized, clockwork joints jammed, stiff fingers offered no resistance. The maiden without hands in the fairy tale found her king through virtue. Adira looked across dim Carcosa, revealed and reflected in her mother's dark eyes. In the landscape of Adira's future, there was no visible king. The yellow tatters that blew in the wind were the shredded labia of the murdered queen, putrescent with the stench of disease. They were the burned clumps of blonde hair billowing from her scalp, the ropey flags of vocal cords torn from her howling throat. The wind silenced her warped song and called another name.

Tough stumps trembled and towered over the corpse of the Yellow Queen in Adira's dreams. Having killed once, she could kill again. Her angel would fight for her. Her angel and she were one and the same, a beautiful creature conjoined in twin acts of violence, one stillborn, one maimed. Adira's eyes rose silently in private darkness to defy the mirror, birthing twin black suns blooming with merciless love.

Deceived by the mirror's silvering, by the space where

time turns inside out; Adira deceived in the realm where dead vipers copulate, and love looks like hate. The queen is alive. The future is old and patient. Time is the winning predator, and every moment spirals deeper into the heart of the beast.

II. LARVA: PARALLEL FLESH

"Being apart gave me time to think," Peter said, in answer to her question. "About us, about our future. What really matters. Witnessing the world in crisis is just, well; it makes it more dire, more clear. That's why I ask now."

Director Bennet ended the embrace as efficiently as possible. They hadn't spoken for almost two weeks since she vetoed Peter's request for more specimens. She hated how it affected the whole team. *Mom and dad are fighting again.* Hearing the gossip over the loud hum of the microwave, she'd skipped lunch ten minutes ago and headed to their meeting early, eager to restore the professional peace. And now this plea for intimacy. Bennet moved across the lab, using a work station and monitor to solidify the barrier between them.

She checked the most recent flow cytometry tests. Her brain couldn't make sense of the data. Peter's proposition lit her mind on fire with too many conflicting emotions.

Avoiding Peter's eyes, Bennet focused blankly on the

monitor. "Three more stages left in this specimen trial, and still there's very little reliable information. No way to predict the viability or outcome of the project. If the outbreak keeps spreading, we have no idea what sort of world we'll be living in nine months from now."

"No one knows the future. That's never stopped the human race from reproducing."

Bennet smirked. "Well, if you're going to make it sound so romantic."

Peter leaned on the opposite side of the work station. Bennet felt the subtle tilt with annoyance. Peter never stopped pushing when he got an idea in his head. He said, "I can't imagine a life with anyone else. I know you want a family, too. We can have that together. Right now. No two people in human history have ever waited for a perfect world. Who knows? Our child might be the one person who will change things for the better if the weapon fails. Nothing improves without taking risks."

"Please, can we stay focused on completing this project before we try to give birth to the next messiah?"

"I'm serious about this. Why are you being flippant?"

As the administrative head in the male-dominated defense project, Bennet fielded constant challenges without including Peter's new penchant for workplace drama. During their mutual silence of the past weeks, tense rumors spread among the engineers and biologists that the higher-ups thought it was too late to impede the outbreak. A sense of futility and rising panic in the bunker undermined Bennet's optimism and authority.

Of course, it was more than the job, but Peter didn't deserve her trust so soon after his last surprise performance. The readings on the monitor blurred. Bennet felt shaky and tearful. "Can we not talk about this now?"

"The future is always uncertain. Now is all that matters."

"Before the surge in fanaticism, I might have said yes." She said it and meant it. Everything about her said yes: her body's readiness, her emotional longing, and her most secret, heartfelt ambitions. Everything said yes except Bennet's intellect. If Peter knew how much she wanted it, he'd never stop pressuring her to share his dream.

Peter wasn't a dreamer, though, and his new passions disturbed Bennet more than the pressure he exerted pursuing them. He was a multi-doctorate specialist in psychology and the cognitive neuroscience of dream states. He knew better than anyone else how high the stakes were now that the world had gone insane.

Bennet measured out her words with care. "I need to maintain my focus, and so do you, on validating the hypothesis, weaning the weapon, and reversing the rampant psychosis. As you pointed out in our staff meeting, the Yellow Sign is a real threat."

"Take a day or two to think it over."

"No. Not in a world rotting from the inside out with slow, quiet, mass hysteria. Not with mad acolytes emptying entire cities."

Bennet didn't exaggerate, and Peter knew it. Tomb-like skyscrapers stood barren, filled with strange, lichenoid growths along the gulf coast from Houston to Baton Rouge to Biloxi, as if diseased ideas took physical root where intelligent life had fled. Former urban residents captured from the wild spoke in altered languages impossible to parse, giving the impression of totemic cannibal cults rising on the outskirts of Galveston and Slidell, mud-worshipers who embedded their children's bodies in sacrificial swamps, mass trials by self-vivisection, communion ceremonies of death and dementia through ingestion of poisonous substances, and a whole host of inhuman, incomprehensible, degrading acts.

Rescue teams were lost, leaving behind garbled broadcasts and dismantled equipment. One black box that was recovered and brought back for analysis exhausted cryptologists. After working with the recording for five days, they appeared stooped and lumbering through the corridors like primates or drunks. They barricaded the audio lab. The black box message blared the bunker's comms. Before the footage went black, the security cam showed four naked figures surrounding a dim yellow grid that spun like a diagram of a tornado. They circled it in a freakish dance, stripping skin from their partners' exposed backs and clothing the holographic fetish at their center. Discordant, ecstatic screams saturated the bunker's sound system for seven full minutes before security bypassed the door. Carnage comparable to a battlefield concealed the remains of only one twisted, tortured body.

The unexplained disappearances, the captive acolytes who vanished from holding cells and treatment centers with no known means of egress and no evidence of suicide or flight; these cases disturbed Bennet the most. If she accepted Peter's theory that the unpredictable entropy of dream states encompassed an extant and separate world that intersected with visible, known reality, the rules of physics and math had ceased to apply. Reason disintegrated with every attack. As long as humans remained fodder and conduit for an otherworldly, malevolent force, Bennet refused to feed her selfish desire for a child.

"When the project moves forward, when the world is back in order, then we'll try again. When there's some sign of hope." Bennet looked up from the monitor and met the challenge of Peter's gaze.

He was inches away, blue eyes blazing. "A child is hope."

"No," she said, "That's wrong-headed. A child is a human being who deserves hope. And safety, and a sane and ordered environment, things we can't offer outside of this bunker."

"Come and look, though! That's the other reason I called you here. We're well on our way into phase two. She's hatched."

"She?"

Peter crossed to the viewing platform for the habitat enclosure in the central lab area and beckoned Bennet to follow. "Forgive my personalization. It's like naming a ship, a bacterium, or a new star. A habit I picked up from my grandfather. Now, come see how much she's grown."

Behind a thick Plexiglas casing coated with an inner layer of alginate hydrogel, lush plants entwined with glass, silk, metals, polyurethane and carbonized branches to form a dense, surreal thicket. Collagen tubing around the circumference of the base provided ventilation and the means to introduce liquid or airborne materials. Flexible built-in sterile gloves allowed sampling by various syringes and manipulation of the EEG electrodes and wires. Suspended in the recesses of the ceiling, cultured cerebral spheroids dangled and pulsated with organic electricity on a synthetic polymer scaffold. Web-like connections already formed threads of tissue between the maturing bio-fabricated orbs. Their neural energy and chemical transmissions provided a potential source of food, augmentation material to be cannibalized, or both. The infant weapon was a new and unknown form of life, dynamic and self-organizing, framed on hybrid mechanized bio-architecture.

"There's my girl. Notice the push for survival, growth, transformation."

Peter gestured toward an azure-toned ball visible through a gap in the humid tangle of plant, synthetic, and cortical tissues. It was the shape and size of an acorn. Where the shell was cracked at the lower tip, a pale, thick worm poked through, chewing with a miniature serrated maw. The larva gnawed the egg and ingested the shell. Its soft body squeezed through brittle blue remains, expanding and contracting to achieve locomotion. The bulky larva was transparent enough for Bennet to witness the progress of azure shards as they succumbed to digestive enzymes. With a microscope, lab techs would witness the commotion of nanomotors quivering inside each cell of the organism, strings of silicon entwined with cultured protein codes containing a programmed life story designed to accelerate cognitive development.

Peter clutched Bennet's arm with a thrill he clearly expected her to share. "Isn't she a beauty?"

Bennet didn't protest his unwelcome grasp. The creature made her sick. Her balance faltered as the squirming larva bloated and gorged on the stem of native hawthorn where it had hatched. It stripped the branch and then moved on to a scrap of steel. Indiscriminate, lacking the hyper-specialization of an insect, the larva proved capable of devouring nearly any material as a food source and incorporating its properties into the larval body. It fed and grew visibly larger during the minutes that passed while Peter and Bennet watched, he in awe, she with revulsion. The larva's omnivorous appropriation reminded Bennet how much of the weapon's materials derived from human models, how much humanoid cortical and glial tissue animated every cell. The sensation that an alert, human consciousness was trapped in the body of a worm appalled her as the larva puffed and convulsed.

"Here we go! She's already preparing to molt." Peter squeezed Bennet's hands in excitement. She squeezed back to be kind and then pulled them away, hiding her hands in the pockets of her lab coat. She took a deep breath, mentally counting to five as she inhaled...and five as she exhaled to affirm her balance, and focused on the feeling of her feet on the solid metal platform.

Peter remained rapt. His theories came to life in the grub's writhing.

The blubbery larva shed its birth skin, inching out thickly, extending to a more rubbery length. The new instar pumped up two sets of false horns, juddering protrusions that framed either end like a pair of pale, jaundiced masks. Bennet didn't know which end of the organism was the face until the fat worm doubled back on its own girth, searched with blind hunger, and swallowed the dead sleeve of infant skin.

ADIRA THE MAD dreamed with her body. She learned how by making love to her dead angel twin instead of wasting away in the hospital after the brutal amputation of her hands. Unusual sense organs possessed her individual particles. A unique consciousness dwelled within each cell. Communicating via electrochemical impulses, thoughts formed tissues, tissues built organs, and organs accreted into a girl of sixteen dragged home cowering under her mother's fist. The stinging aftermath of the slap bruised less than the message of the curse whispered earlier beside the sanctuary of her hospital bed: "I'll get your body back. I don't care how. I'll bury you in summer, in sunlight, beneath the full buck moon."

The shock of truth, systemic signals stronger than her mother's spoken law. Adira's face burned.

The fist opened to give comfort. The curse softened into seduction. "I love you, honey. It's my job to take care of you. You can't even feed yourself with these."

Circling Adira's silver hands with spiny claws, her mother slipped the intricate prosthetics off and exposed Adira's raw stumps. The wounds oozed yellow putrescence in answer to the poison in the dragon's touch. Adira's twin angel huddled in the corner, wings tight like fists, weeping with Adira. The angel ate the boy and possessed enough power to secrete silver clockwork hands, functional things of beauty, cleverly crafted and cleanly affixed to substitute for Adira's stolen limbs; why did it cry? Why didn't it fight?

"These precious things are too valuable for you to play with. They belong on display. We can't have them clunking around and getting damaged. Besides, someone might steal them from you. How would you defend yourself?"

"My sister."

Adira gestured at the fading angel with one of her tattered stumps. Stricken, shaking as much as Adira's arm, her mother turned away from the china cabinet where she locked up the silver hands. The scuffed baroque was too massive for the small mobile home. Its horned shadow loomed over the waning angel. By the time Adira's mother faced the strange incarnation of her miscarriage, the angel was no more than a stain on aging carpet.

Black satisfaction bloomed in her mother's eyes. "You're sick and seeing things, honey. The best cure is hard work."

Adira's body melted. For a moment, she had seen fear under the dragon's mask. Her many minds searched for a cellular equation to upset the oppressive balance of her eternal return to the same fixed state. Mother plus boy equals Carcosa. Angel plus hands equals Carcosa. Adira minus hands, divided by boy equals Carcosa. Boy divided by angel, equals Adira plus hands, divided by mother equals Carcosa.

From the still, dark pools of her mother's eyes, across the windless lakes in the lost land of Carcosa, the Yellow Queen arose like an impulse to scream.

"What's the matter, honey? Are you sad you couldn't make your husband happy?"

Adira swallowed the scream like a long, oiled rope, ingesting another inch or two each day. It stuck in her throat, dangling out like an extra tongue, tangling her words and slurring them into nonsense.

Service to the Yellow Queen became easier once Adira accepted that she was a puppet in a play. The cramped mobile home was the cardboard castle Carcosa. The tasks assigned Adira set the stage for the entrance of an outsider in a pallid mask. As Adira worked harder, her mother slept more and more and ate less and less. The bones of her mother's face assumed a veneer of pale prominence, suggesting the outsider was already there, had always been there, and that the mask was the revelation of her mother's true face. Adira studied how the cycle of the play functioned. Obedience and abstinence were not requirements as much as unmitigated facts in a closed loop. The tattered marionette Adira followed her skull-mother's advice and kept her stumps clean.

The harsh lye abraded them. On occasions when she was well enough, her mother scrubbed. "If you're dirty, the devil can come and take you."

Adira donned the long sleeves of shame her mother sewed shut to hide that she was a poorly made puppet, the shoddy job of some hack. Tasks simple with fingers, simpler with her clockwork silver hands, grew as cumbersome as fat. Her clumsy stumps burned with constant chafing, making it difficult to lever any object within their blunt grasp. Adira used her mouth for precise operations. Keys pursed between her lips, packages torn open with her teeth, tongue typing texts and dialing her mother's doctor. She cleaned countertops with a spray bottle hugged to her chest, leaned over to direct it with an uncomfortable hunch, pumped the too-small handle with her free forearm often missing her target, then tossed a rag down she carried clenched in her teeth and rubbed with her less abraded elbows. Mopping involved a similar maneuver. Adira scrubbed the floors wearing wet socks, stepping in and out of the soap bucket until the flesh on her feet puckered from damp.

Rags in her hair, rags in her eyes, rags in her mouth, the wet puppet made mute gestures of obeisance. Citrus, pine, and bleach, homeopathic cures for the deadly poison and sickening smell that oozed from her mother's room. Missed doctor's appointments, relentless messages from specialists, and unfinished prescriptions angered the skeleton woman, who desired only darkness. Giddy with the toxicity of endless tasks, Adira circled the sickbed in a flat trance of obedience.

Health revealed infractions and failings. The skeleton woman stood over Adira, urging her and holding her hair back in an unusual moment of lucid strength. Later, she re-washed the dinner dishes that Adira didn't get clean enough. "School's starting soon. You need to watch your weight if you want anyone to ask you out. You don't want to miss the homecoming dance, do you?"

Adira's mother bent down to get a sponge from under the sink. Her skirt caught in the tight, precise apron bow tied behind her back. From her exposed vagina, a fleshy tip poked out and nosed around the cleft between her thighs. Always slender, the skeleton woman had grown more emaciated with every passing day. The tendril wasn't able to find any fat. After one tentacle slid out in its slow search, a second one followed, less furtive. Soon three starry fingers slathered across the room at Adira. Twelve foot long tentacles smeared the floor with mucus, twined around Adira's neck, stung her with toothy suction cups, and nudged the softest parts of Adira's flesh.

Her pores dilated with panic. The nodes probed into the microscopic consciousness of Adira's internal codes. She blacked out into another dimension where the starry fingers were instruments of intelligence, capable of reshaping reality through gestures incomprehensible to the gathering of cells organized as a human brain. The architecture of isolating neurons in a bowl on top of a body was laughable to them, if indeed they laughed. It was like locking a congregation inside a church, where the fires of faith smoldered in dead works.

The blind, all-seeing appendages flooded her with fulsome ruminations: an atmospheric effect of extreme weather, the cosmic afterglow of a distant sun's death-storm. Emotional urgency swelled on the gel-like tips of the yellow tentacles and pressed fire into her adipose tissue, depositing self-aware bullets of swollen putrescence.

The electrical charge of alien thoughts ripped Adira open with a subcutaneous symphony of unreason. Bees buzzed beneath her skin. Nothing was real, everything was real. Every improbable world existed in her hot flesh. This world and the next, all the worlds that came before: Carcosa, Hastur, and Hali, meaningless names signifying the ineffable, neither person nor place nor god, but hybrid, multiform, and formless. Devouring names seeding insanity in Adira's dreaming cells.

Puppet perceptions lost meaning in the greater universe. The strong, soft tentacles lifted Adira by the neck, and with joyous disintegration her mind shook apart and spread through the rest of her body, brain dripping down in shattered globules, filling her with the black wisdom of idiocy, rising up in gold tears that drowned her button eyes. Her vision went liquid. Her body was a maelstrom of minds. The nub of a thick tendril bulged with yellow mucous and slipped inside her and swelled. She thrust at it, pungent and warm, dancing marionette, and swallowed the otherworldly arm. Unthinking, she tugged and extracted the starry organism from the cleft of its companion lair. Two more tentacles followed, slipping, prodding, and then disappearing inside her, consumed by Adira's instinctive thirst.

The stranglehold on her neck went slack. Adira sucked down the last writhing arm with a wet slap.

Startled by the sound, her mother swung around.

She yanked her knotted skirt. "Why didn't you tell me I was standing here bare-assed? Get up and put these dishes away. Do I have to do everything in this house myself? "

The twin black suns of her mother's eyes burned in accusation. Adira burst out in shameless laughter. The hidden, hairless, empty eye she'd seen seared deeper, more blind and hungry than any lover or foe. Adira tripped the burning circle and laughed harder. Unblinking, a seeker from afar peered across time, fever dreaming in silence, evolving, lying in wait like a weapon in heat.

◎

THE HABITAT'S modular components were in full use after three weeks of molts. Peter prepared the team for an emergency build. "We'll know we're out of the woods when she becomes lethargic. She'll stop eating, climb higher, and begin construction of the chrysalis. Believe me, too much growth is a good problem for us to have."

Nine feet long, segmented and thick, the giant larva moved with writhing convulsions like an active intestine. Three sets of prolegs on its rear grasped a stripped beam. It hung upside down, gnawing. The wide, oval maw gaped below a circle of horn-like protrusions that formed a wobbly crown on top of an eyeless head. Sets of serrated teeth spiraled in opposite directions, grinding carbon-based matter, minerals, and synthetics into digestible nutrition. The omnivorous capability of the hybrid organic machine proved surprising in scope, even to Peter.

"If she can metabolize such an unusual variety of materials, she'll grow the armor of a tank." He programmed an extra meal of plant fibers and metal alloys to populate the feed chute. The larva squirmed toward the sound of fingers on the keyboard.

Peter's attachment to the weapon worried Director Bennet. She felt compelled to keep him in check. "Let's remember to be objective with our expectations, and our pronouns. You said it best yourself, we're growing a weapon, not a pet."

"But think about military dogs. A good relationship makes them more effective. We're going to learn a whole new way of thinking and perceiving when she communicates with us."

"Police dogs can't be pets or companions. You can't have it both ways. You have to be prepared to see your work destroyed in battle. Or lost somewhere, devoured in some realm we may never understand. Sacrificing the weapon may be the only way humanity wins."

Peter gazed beyond Bennet into the habitat where the worm-like creature rhythmically fed. "She's strong. A unique object of beauty. A truly new form of life. She may grow into what the ancients called a seraph. With her advanced cognition, she won't be bound in space and time the way we are. Consider the possibilities. Maybe she met our ancestors long ago. Maybe humanity is irrelevant if she survives."

His voice was hushed with awe. No one knew how the madness spread. Suspicion and anger wafted like a cold wind through Bennet's chest. Her throat tightened. Three weeks ago Peter wanted to have a baby with her. How dare he say humanity was irrelevant? How dare he? Bennet froze. Her disproportionate anger shocked her back to reality. She recognized she was overreacting. If Peter was growing delusional, the worm of insanity might also wriggle inside her gut.

She forced a smile. "You anthropomorphize too much. Remember when we lost the jade plant?"

"You told me I shouldn't name him." Peter turned to Bennet with no threat of a dark thrall in his expression. A spark of amusement brightened his eyes. "I admit it. I have a bit of the 'savage' in me, as my grandfather used to say. I know the terminology is coarse, but he used it with great affection. Don't we all? When we break everything down to the particle level—"

Bennet's sigh of relief came out louder than she intended. Peter stopped mid-sentence and rubbed her shoulder. "Perhaps it's time to wrap up for tonight. You look drained."

She tilted her head toward his hand. "Drained and wilted. Nearing jade plant intensity."

They'd been down in the bunker for more than two months straight. Bennet craved the sight of the mountain sky. She needed to feel her feet touch the earth, not tunnel through dirt encased in steel and concrete. Ten days apart had changed her. Peter had no idea what she'd been through. "Let's go up for a few days. I can rush the security clearance. We'll do a day hike."

"Spotty service in the mountains or I'd consider it."

"I think the rest of the team can handle her for a couple of hours. You won't be out of range for long. We need to talk."

Peter pulled away to close his file and leave his monitor to lapse into sleep mode. The giant grub chewed and writhed behind him in the habitat, pale and yellow under artificial lights. When he came back to Bennet, he cupped both of her shoulders. "We do? Talk about what?"

Bennet leaned against Peter, put her forehead on his cheek, and brushed his neck with her mouth. He smelled fresh and exciting, like a bud about to flower, an intimation of a storm. For a moment, she didn't care if anyone walked in on them. "Let's go up to Cheyenne for a hike. We need more air, more light. What do you say?"

Budding deep inside, soft tentacles twisting, exploring and easing through displaced veins, pushing through pockets of adipose tissue, squirming through her lower intestines and jiggling her bladder and bowels. Adira missed school.

Tentacles took root. Control came close to a complete forfeit. Adira digested the message of the tentacles and their dream-wave rising. Rising like giant breakers, cascading over boundaries as if Adira were a ship and her tongue the storm-lashed deck, the motion of the mind beyond the hairless portal of the solitary hidden eye crashing in and out, up and down, until the stringy wriggling worm thoughts broke out. Fever smashing like glass threads, a million eager maggots, Adira vomited up the odor of burnt chocolate and neglected meat.

Nothing solid came up. Mere maggot breath.

Within Adira, a million white bodies wriggled, as though she'd become a bag of fleshy worms, a thin sheet of cellophane wrapped around carnage pleading to burst. Meat turned to juice, pink muscle froth flowed for hungry larvae. Bowels churned, unable to void. *Who are we?* they asked and demanding with insistent head capsules, bodies molting, shedding, and shimmering away, born as flies.

Black colony swarming in heat, black maggots rubbing legs and eyes, black fever mating legs and eyes, summer fever mating black and laying, laying, and mating and dying. Flies like flowers bloomed from her eyes.

Flowers in her hair, flowers in her eyes, flowers in her mouth; eight thousand black maggot identities born into the stinking air and bled dry in stinking lies. Dream-flies, dead too quick to answer, dead too quick to die, alive, alive; leaving trails behind like ghosts. Smoke-fingers feeling for Adira in her habitat. Fingers of the Yellow Queen.

Yellow in her habitat, yellow in her bed. Dehydrated and stuffed, larval and lucid. Adira, dreamed: "I am always awake."

Her grub-like body helpless and hanging in the lab, she clung to the branches of neural spheroids that pulsed with electrochemical excess and networked through her puffy pale flesh. Swarms of flies, swarms of eyes, swarms of ideas. Helpless, handless, lifted like a balloon inflated by jaundiced yellow breath.

Cradled by the Yellow Queen, who held the nine-foot-long grub in her arms and spoke soft love-words to the pusillanimous, incapable flesh, to the puffed-up worm that cried from a distant vortex. The queen's cloak in tatters, blown by harsh wind. Gusts roared with song and tore at her cloak, tore away the mantle of her skin, flayed her putrescent yellow flaps, unwound the lie of permanence. The queen in tatters, bones of her arms pressing into the overgrown maggot, moist with yellow pus. The sound of it squirmed as it soiled itself; the sound of a soft body seeking for something on which to feed.

The queen, all bones, brought the maggot up the ladder of her ribs. She held its orifice below her collarbone. The maggot's mouthparts sucked on the queen's ribs and sternum, suckling, nudging, searching. The unstructured mass of the larva pressed through skeletal cavities like industrial spray foam and filled the spaces between the bones. Fat grub flesh adorned the queen with meat.

The fluorescent yellow of infection stained Adira's sheets. Her sleeves were stiff with the dried discharge leaking from her un-scrubbed stumps. Her wounds had slathered the bed through her shirt, dripped down the mattress, and splattered the walls as she thrashed. She didn't know how long she'd convalesced, or why her mother had let her wallow. Adira felt no pain in her stumps. With black gangrene fear, she ripped off her shirt.

In place of her wounds, two fully functional mouths. Adira thought of her phantom fingers, and the lips pursed and sneered. She imagined tickling, and a tongue lolled out. She opened and closed the mouths and swallowed their saliva, dripping. She licked the lips and tongued the clefts in the teeth, failing. Perhaps it took practice to stop them from drooling. Or maybe, since Adira had slept so long, the newborn orifices were eager to feed.

Flowers in her hands, flowers in her mouth, flesh flowers feeding in a mercy of wounds.

BENNET GRABBED Peter's arm when his foot slid on an incline covered with rubble. He looked tired and sallow under the natural light. Open air didn't suit him like it used to. For a moment, she set aside the thrill of climbing higher that grew for her with every step. "Do you need to rest a bit? We can stop."

"I'm fine." Peter regained his footing. He looked at the ground as if seeking the source of betrayal.

"We should head back after we reach the summit. It's been a long day. We're so close, though! Through that clearing right up ahead. Do you see?"

Peter looked up. "Ah, yes, I see. More trees and rocks."

Bennet tried to muster more encouragement than disappointed. "Come on, don't be like that. Once we make it there, we'll be in the clouds, like standing in the sky."

He smiled and showed her the light in his eyes that she longed for. "The queen of heaven on her magic carpet."

She leaned in to kiss him when Peter's smile became a wince. He released his arm from hers and pressed two fingers into his ribs. "You go ahead. All those weeks below ground are taking their toll. Ouch."

Bennet stayed beside him, concerned. Peter said, "Go ahead. I know you hate losing your momentum."

"You sure you're okay? Nothing serious?"

"A cramp. Need to catch my breath. Right behind you."

"Okay," she said. "I'll come back and make sure you're still alive if you're not there in an hour or two."

Peter did his best impression of a laugh. "I love you, too. No, go on."

Bennet turned her back and bounded upward. Peter crouched over the sore spot in his ribs. He waited for the pain to subside, a small act of faith in the midst of an accreting darkness only Bennet still believed they could stop. Her head spun with myriad thoughts. Leaving the lab abandoned and betrayed, trying to keep pace with an ever-growing black spiral, she worried what would happen if Peter became unfit. The way he clutched his side seeded an image in her mind of his weapon clutching at wounds, bleeding, weeping, wounding again; feeding on intermittent slaughter and incessant release. Bennet reached the summit and reeled at the multiplicity and magnificence of a being that gorged on destruction: the impossible promise of transmutational technology akin to magic, weapon as energy, one as many.

The altitude cleared her head. The sky glowed with a benevolent sunset. Footsteps and rustling branches warned of Peter's ascent up the trail. Bennet despised feeling anxious when he approached. She had to trust him. She didn't want a future founded on a lie. It was time to come clean.

Bennet called down in a conversational tone, though she kept her back to Peter as he glimpsed her on the peak. "I was going to talk to you about this before you brought it up, but the problem is I'd already made my decision. When we were apart for a couple of weeks. I couldn't find a way to say it to you. Not underground like that, where you can't see any light, any hope. It's great up here, isn't it? The world feels real. It makes sense. Do you know what I mean?"

Peter stumbled. The sun sank lower. Silence retreated behind the impenetrable wall of pines in the canyon below. Confusion hovered in the clouds gathering above. Grey pigment stained the hardened cumulus peaks. Neon pink and orange shocked the soft underbellies. Peter felt the shock bloom dimly in his consciousness. He didn't know what part of him was hardened, what part stained, what part fell endlessly through the black spiral they shared. He didn't know if he'd heard Bennet right. "What…what are you trying to tell me?"

"I knew it wasn't the right time. I don't have any

regrets, except I should have told you sooner." Bennet spoke to the sky, not quite able to look at Peter. Not yet. She shifted her weight from one strong leg to the other like a pent up mare, looked down, and gave the ground a demonstrative stomp. "Places like this give me strength. Don't you feel it? This air, this altitude, this unmolested dirt. I had a TA in grad school with family ties to the land out here. She told me I was 'like the mountain' in front of the class; we were doing some touchy-feely team exercise. God, it embarrassed me. I didn't feel like a mountain. I was a child, a fish out of water trying to prove I could swim. Or fly. I mean, obviously fish can swim, right?"

She pivoted to face Peter and planted her feet. "My fellowship was the only thing standing in between me and the trailer park. Maybe a mental hospital. I didn't have it easy growing up. I realize how hard this is for you. I haven't told you much about my past. I put it behind me. But a child, now, with the world exploding into mass psychosis? No way. It's too much."

"A child?"

Bennet nodded. "That's what I wanted to tell you. Why we came here."

Peter looked around the stretch of wilderness below as if it might offer an explanation less difficult to grasp. Somnolent in the dense growth, a muffled wind breathed between the trees and stole Peter's labored sigh. "Whose is it? Is it mine?"

"Don't be like that."

Peter edged closer to Bennet. "Don't I get any say in the matter?" Shadows felt for cover across the valley.

Treetops succumbed to darkness. He took another step closer. "How far along?"

"No EKG, no myelin, no consciousness; nothing a scientist like you, nothing any educated person calls life." Her eyes faltered and her throat strained. She felt foolish, near tears. "I grieve for it, though. I held a voice inside my body, and I had to let it go, and this is something almost sacred that you can never share, never understand."

The pain rooted in Peter's side spread to his chest. A giant's hand grew inside his body and squeezed his ribs, lungs, and esophagus. He fought against the pressure, stealing enough oxygen to protest. "And you decided to tell me this now, why? To prove what, exactly? Just to find out how much you could hurt me?"

"This isn't about you." Bennet's tears dried with outrage. "You weren't there. I didn't know if I'd ever see you again."

Peter closed his eyes. The pain within him, unknown to Bennet, focused into one thin, ephemeral thread. A wounded, three-legged spider dangled from the silk tendril, one tiny spiral within the greater, spiraling abyss. "You're afraid."

"Of course I'm afraid. Reality is under attack. Pockets of our civilization have already crumbled, and we don't understand why. We're not even sure who or what the enemy is yet."

Peter's gut coiled in a spring, a tight trap of spider silk. Whether he laid the trap or had become ensnared in it, he didn't know. He knew only the raw sensitivity of the woven matrix that trembled with the tug of prey stuck under his skin, the signal of tense threads that told him the time neared to pounce.

He was shaking, cold. She didn't seem to notice. "No. You're afraid of who you are. That's the problem. That's why you drag me through your atrocities. You're afraid to fly."

Near the edge of the summit, Bennet took a hesitant step toward Peter. "Hey, there's no rush. We can try again later. I just don't want to make the same mistakes my parents made, okay?"

Twilight turned Peter's bright blue eyes to dark grey. "You lack faith. I have enough faith for both of us, for an army. We will grow an army. I've seen it. I'm ready. I have found the Yellow Sign."

Bennet recoiled. Peter glared. He stood in her path, breathing faster than normal. She realized he shouldn't still be winded by now, that something was wrong. His shoulders hunched and shuddered. His hands clenched. There was no way down except past him or over the cliff. Bennet lunged. Peter leapt. With the thrust of the giant's fist, he launched their bodies over the ledge and they tumbled as one tangled creature with many legs spiraling down through the pine-darkened abyss.

UNDULATING FROM ITS SPINNERET, the monstrous larva weaved a mat of slender gold and copper threads as it hung suspended in mid-air. With its last meal disgorged, the soft body conjured dreams. Seeking images of flight, it opened and closed its curious pores. Sensations of weight hurled from a great height, of weightlessness and lifting, of displaced air that howled toward sudden landings. Drifting, falling sensations fluttered inside its elastic skin. Chemical pulses of electricity excited the neural circuitry woven through its organs. Then it stilled.

The skin hardened. Glands ceased to spin. Immobile, the large grub's exterior stiffened like pliable wax over a fluid center. Inside the cocoon, its contents liquefied further, reorganizing cellular and cognitive structures into trident and diamond shapes. Patterns bloomed like crystals, increasing a network of exponential links. The minds inside the chrysalis broiled with manic activity as the shell turned grey, static, and silent.

Dreaming, Adira awoke with hungry hands.

III. PUPA: MUTILATION PSALM

Soaring down in terror, out of control, wind ripping wings to shreds, ground so far, how far, how soon to death? Adira's many mouths snapped and bit at racing air. Nothing to grasp in her fast descent. Dread of ground, groundless, prayer for impact, falling through a dream-gulch, a grave with no bottom, a spiral with no center of gravity, her disordered orbit in endless space, her circle seduced and split.

She sank like a heavy leaf spinning, a leaf like a rock, like a carcass, like her lost slabs of flesh. What happened to her hands when the boy took them? Where did they go after falling to the floor like dead fish? They hadn't gasped or grasped in asphyxiating throes of death, but rather lay compliant and soft, clay begging for an imprint. Wads of weak wounded flesh.

Adira shot into sophomore year like flowers vomited from a black hole. As she sunbathed naked and many-mouthed on the roof of the mobile home, the fat summer sun settled into autumn and engulfed the sky. The yellow orb of fire filled her with light and longing. It burned closer, bigger, and brighter the more lavishly she licked with her hungry tongues, feeding and fattening the mouths on her own juices, mothering them with fire from the sky. The yellow sun spread enormous and opened wide with flames of teeth. Once she slipped inside, the supernova blaze collapsed into famished blackness, engulfing Adira in its starved center. Empty blackness burned like the twin black suns setting in her mother's eyes.

Death in dim Carcosa.

Lost in her mother's eyes, she fell to the astonished land through the mirror's silvered side, where no stars reflected in the flat circle of the lake.

The queen languished in bed, eyes burning hollow with hate in her skull-like face. Gorgon eyes judged Adira thanklessly as she nursed her mother's failing health. Irrational emotions with unknown names blasted her. Horrified hope electrified her with grief. The impossible exit of the queen from the stage loomed with despairing delight.

The gorgon skull opened its fire-blackened eyes. "Get some decent clothes on. You have to go back to school."

"I don't think I should leave."

"Make sure you keep your stumps covered. The devil can take you—"

"Yeah, yeah. The devil will take me if I'm dirty. I know."

"Don't sass back, young lady."

Adira hid her mouths from her mother. She let them get very dirty. They bounced against a river of bodies, flowing through institutional corridors. Trampling her feet, crushing her soft stomach against the hard sill of a window, uncontrollable empathy bled milk from Adira's every pore. Suckling things sensed the moisture in her receptive flesh. Boys with devil-dog eyes squeezed the warm sponge of her behind. Girls in smirking lipstick prodded the tender pulse in her neck. Calculating things, relentless things; no was impossible after one hesitant yes. They took turns, traded her, and drained every teat on her sore chest.

Pushing, crushing, laughing, the class funneled Adira toward an unknown wing of the campus. Through an old locker room, she entered a neglected indoor swimming pool. Pond scum greened stagnant water thick enough to hold up a littering of dead leaves. Stray notebook paper and crumpled candy wrappers sparkled with broken glass. Windows smashed around the perimeter wept with intruding vines. In the shallow end of the pool, muddy water eddied in a circle one inch deep. The overgrown vines branched across the deep end and rooted in the murk, seeking fresh cracks in the tiles to plunder. The green arteries reached for two pale, blubbery objects abandoned in the shallow end where a trickle deposited trash.

The flow of filthy water led Adira to her lost hands.

They looked like fakes. She might have mistaken them for rubber props if she hadn't known a sudden, visceral, intimate tug, as if her severed parts longed to return. Bloated from disuse and osmosis, the pudgy things bobbed in the meager liquid with deluded animation. Three gangrenous fingertips tangled in a bruised mockery of human touch.

Adira dropped to her knees, leaning, weeping, her lost limbs moored out of reach.

MIGRAINE-BLACK PAIN PIERCED Bennet's temple and woke her from an insensate lull. The dream was like swallowing dark sludge. Sensation lingered beyond her memory of its facts. What was Peter talking about?

"You killed me."

Her vision a black spiral, Director Bennet's head soared over the cliff ledge and crashed through a sieve of trees. Unable to gain purchase on the loose rocks, the grappling momentum of two bodies speeded her disastrous slide. Opening her eyes where she came to rest in the canyon, her stomach lurched. The woods hurled her to and fro like a carnival ride.

Bennet sank back. She closed her eyes. Peter eased her head onto a pillow of moss.

After gentleness, his words were a baffling assault. "I don't know how to worship you anymore. Maybe that's the whole point of your Arcanum, though I admit I still cling to some pithy pride in the work I've done to parse it. I'll finish what needs to be done, and then everything ends. Unless you've deceived the constellations about that, too." He faltered. Exhausted tears interrupted his complaint. "You can feast on my corpse. Feed me to the black watchdog, kill me at the gate. Kill me as many times as you like."

Bennet struggled between the cold terror growing in her chest, anger rising in the heat of her breath, and a confused maternal yearning to ease Peter's pain. "I think I missed something, or maybe I forgot something when I fell." She didn't mention why she fell, didn't voice the accusation. "Help me out here. Did I say something strange when I was asleep?"

"I'll keep you safe long enough to pilot the weapon. I can't promise any more than that. I can't begin to fathom your demands."

Bennet barely recognized Peter's strangled affect. She repeated his name like an incantation, hoping to call him back from beyond the wall of delusion. "Peter, I'm injured. I can't pilot anything. All I want is for you to help me. Peter, help me find a path and walk. Will you do that?"

"My God, can you stop being so disingenuous?" He threw his face into his hands, moaning and rocking.

Bennet's eyes were wide open. The woods around her had ceased to spin. She didn't risk sitting up, saved her energy for later. She saw she was going to need it. "Everything is going to be okay, Peter. I promise." He huddled and wept. She stretched out a comforting hand. He was almost out of reach. Her mind lurched. She pushed away a rotten memory from the missing dream and focused on the present, on Peter. "Let's think this through together, okay? I'm not trained for neuro-tactical combat. Piloting is for soldiers and generals, right? If you think I'm the best person, though, I'll do it. I trust you, Peter. I'll need a lot of training, so we need to get back to the lab as soon as we can. Peter, my phone is gone. Do you have yours?"

Peter turned and yelled with incredulity. "You test me and you test me, over and over again, as if you think you can break me. You must know by now you have broken me utterly. The sigil may be madness, but it is also revelation." Then he laughed, looking past Bennet as if some wild amusement frolicked at a distance through the shifting foliage of the looming trees. "Sweet ecstasy of torture, you have broken me on the black wheel of the Yellow Sign."

"Peter, this isn't you. You designed the weapon to fight madness. Dreams are infecting reality. I felt it too, when I woke up. You're confused. We'll get you help. We'll find a path out of here. Peter, listen: if we don't get back to the lab soon, there might be nothing left to fight for."

Peter moved closer to Bennet. He stroked her hair and searched her face with watchful eyes. Their azure blue remained grey under the darkened sky. Instead of a bright moon in their firmament, each offered an eclipse. He closed his eyes and pressed his lips to hers. The taste of him conjured a familiar commotion of intimacy. His tongue slid into her mouth. His fingers tangled in the thick hair at the nape of her neck. Tongues circled like vulnerable creatures in heat. Injuries didn't matter anymore. His hands gravitated toward her arousal. The heat hit her with a strong pulse. She wanted him.

He pulled away. She gasped.

"Do you feel that? The emptiness at the center of it all. Nothing left. You killed me when you killed our baby."

Bennet spat away his deceptive kiss. Poisoned, her vision swirled more violently than before. She hugged the ground and suppressed the need to vomit through force of will. Peter crossed his arms and lay down beside her on his back, looking up through the canopy of trees. "You play strange games. You'll pilot the weapon because you must. Your name means strength, in case you didn't know that. That was my first clue, and why I named the weapon after you. I took some liberties with the material in your diary to increase the threat simulation response, but overall, Adira's programmed to synchronize wave and chemical spikes with your unique cell activity patterns."

"After me? I've never kept a diary."

"Of course you didn't. Yet you clearly left it out for me to find. It was impossible to ignore. That very distinctive yellow binding. On the front cover, and crawling up the spine, there it was, asymmetrical and black. The three-pronged spiral sign. The sign spinning like an incessant drill bit, boring into my eyes, night after night. That yellow binding with raw tattered edges, unraveling like a lost herald, an invitation to ineffable battle, to worship, to behold the unknown."

Dazed with disbelief and sickened by excess saliva, Adira Bennet abandoned all pretense of patience. "It's a blank journal. You hallucinated. There's nothing there but my math homework." She was surprised to hear herself screaming. "I never even finished it!"

Peter tilted his head. His tears were gone, his tone cold and resigned. Bennet assumed the burden of tears, balking at his lunatic words. "When this is done, I don't expect to survive in any corporeal sense. I say this before all the unnamed creatures crawling blind from the foreign shores of our lost eternity: I know her. I have seen the Queen in Yellow. Her progeny is my gift to the void."

In chrysalis phase, the weapon wore dormancy's mask. Nine feet long, warmed by artificial light, fattened on an omnivorous diet of synthetic and organic substances, the bulbous grub pupated in the sanctum of the underground laboratory bunker. Sensitive equipment detected aspiration from the biofabrication's porous spiracles. It monitored neuroelectrical pulses from cortical and glial cells that networked through muscular and connective tissues. The body was wired with thinking and processing motors, like a brain. The body was designed to dream.

The weapon mimicked death. An external self-hypnotic immobility reflex concealed intense activity within the hardened coating. Enzymes self-digested and rearranged the larval body. Proteins fed on their remains. Memories embedded in the pupating tissues unraveled and recombined to form new organs with extra-sensory and trans-sensory perception. Cell formations articulated a network of duplicates: eyes that saw inside many minds and those that peered across galaxies; muscles primed to fight history's current battle, while other arcane ligaments stretched with invincible tenacity far enough to defy time. Senses unknown to earthly bodies, impossible to enumerate, recorded in the roots of thought, the multilingual voices of a planet's motion, the rhythm of endless expressions from which life was born.

Maturation opened a positive void.

The book of Adira opened. The aging spine split. New wings parted like the pages of an ancient map, and as a pelvis fractured in childbirth, the symmetrical infection of order strung her tendrils through the invisible universe. The universe willingly expanded to accommodate. The weapon enjoyed the elastic sensation of exploring the boundaries of being and nothingness, the pleasures of playing with dimensions, identities, and time.

All this excitement got her into the mood to hatch.

SHE CRIED on the broken edge of the shallow end. Tears trickled down to the bloated, rotten things. They floated like slugs, yellowing in the algae-crusted water, stinking more than the anaerobic slime that skimmed the neglected surface. She wept without relief. No magic sprang from her tears. No healing balm revived her dead hands.

The pool room was hot. Stagnant water burdened the air. Unintelligible voices murmured behind her, voices like thick whispers bubbling up from the deep end, bubbling and sniggering, pelting her with insults. Gangrene-colored welts bloomed on Adira's skin. Her soft flesh bruised where the words *slut* and *pig* hit and sank in. The class congregated behind her as she kneeled. The hall of cracked windows writhed with their shadows.

From the opposite end of the pool's edge, nails tapped on tile. A dark corner inverted, rounded into a convex mass, and stretched limbs and nose forward like thick smoke. Taking shape from shadow, a small black dog sprang out and trotted up to Adira, eye level with her sobs. It licked her face and nudged her bruises. As the mob closed in around her back, the black dog hopped down into the mire. Quick as oysters, it swallowed Adira's amputated hands.

The black dog barked. Adira had nowhere to run.

Fingers were on her, sharp and firm. Hands hoisted her from behind onto a poolside slab. The crowd of students pummeled her bruises and held down her arms, legs, torso, neck. Strong hands covered her mouth. Adira struggled. A foot slipped free, instantly recaptured. She evaded one grasp to meet another. She was outnumbered. Her mouths screamed and bit. She drew blood. Laughing hands replaced the injured and held her firm.

Faces leered with anticipation. Panting from above polluted the air, mocking Adira's arduous breaths with their hot, hateful taste. Her tongue felt coated in it. The sound of the dog's barking echoed off the hard tiles and lofted ceiling. The shrill, sonorous repetition resounded at a distance until the dog was silenced into a submissive whine. The instructor had arrived.

Clad in a heavy rubber apron and a belt holstering his tools, he contemplated Adira's forcefully splayed form. Strolling at an unhurried pace, he evaluated different angles around the slab. Adira stopped squirming. He didn't look hostile. If only she could catch his eye. The furrows in his face spoke of heavy burdens, unwanted knowledge. He didn't appear older than any other teacher, yet the gravity of his expression, the inescapable thundercloud of his presence, suggested he'd lived for a very long time. Her dark bruises throbbed. Her flesh sensed internal calculations behind his assessing eyes. His eyes, his eyes, she tried to signal his eyes.

Calm and diligent, he dodged her gaze. He nodded once. His head inclined toward her right side.

The class pressed Adira's right bicep and forearm flat

and firm on the concrete platform. She started to writhe and squeal again. The instructor went through his tools. After testing several blades, he selected a large handled cutlet cleaver from his belt. He raised the cleaver thoughtfully and aimed at Adira's elbow joint. With one swing, he hacked her arm half through. Then he leaned in and pressed the embedded cleaver, working it back and forth through the rough gristle and bone. The elbow joint popped apart. Adira threw up in her clamped mouth.

Her forearm fell free. There was still a mouth where her hand should be, silenced and drooling, with cracked teeth. She couldn't feel or taste it. She couldn't fight, she couldn't think, she couldn't scream.

The students hauled the limp girl to the edge of the slab to provide better leverage for the next cut. Adira sprayed vomit through their fingers and gurgled useless protest into disgusted, muffling hands. Demonstrating an expert technique of swift, firm pressure, the teacher braced Adira's shoulder at a sharp angle on the slab and bent her arm back. It snapped out of joint with a sickening crack. He sawed vigorously through the surrounding loose skin and fascia, ripped off the severed limb, and tossed it. Bloody meat slapped and slid across the tile.

Adira's body was a madhouse on fire, a place she could not stay. Her shoulder socket screamed. The shock of pain and integrity's absence forced her mind to shut down. Except her mind kept working and paying attention. Kept staying conscious when a reasonable mind knew it was better to go blank. Her mind refused to obey her body's logic.

Blood-drenched, hot and cold, pouring sweat and shivering, Adira smelled the stench of a soiled toilet and the clean ore of blood. If only they would clean her. She released a runny mash, unable to keep her body sane. The crowd shifted her position on the slab, and the warm fecal paste molded between the cleft of her thighs.

With systematic dexterity, the instructor then removed Adira's other arm as the attentive students held her convulsing parts in place for him. She lost too much blood to stay alive. What remained of her jerked with involuntary awareness. Elbow split, then shoulder of the left arm; ankles severed one by one, knees cracked in half. Each femur bone forced out of its pelvic socket, broken, and detached.

Her copious wounds didn't bleed away consciousness. She counted. Legs and arms cut into ten parts. The instructor deliberated over her torso. He worked to split her back and breast meat, but Adira's hard sternum resisted blow after blow. The students flipped her over. Concrete hit her face. The butcher placed a cold chisel at the base of her spine, and hammered with a separate implement. Her sacrum cracked. Pain shot up her back. He wrenched the splitter up her spine, and fists shoved apart her stubborn sides. Her organs sloshed out in a hot stench.

The butcher caught his breath and stroked her forked neck. He leaned down to finally meet Adira's eyes. He nodded sagely, satisfied that she was awake. He reared up. With one last hard hack her head flew off the slab. It bashed into tile, crushed her nose, and bruised her cheek.

Class was dismissed. The master butcher wiped his tools clean and led them to the exit.

Fight or flight fantasies fractured Adira's disembodied head. Agony without agency. She smelled the ammoniac green mildew on the tile, and hurt her eyes on the glare of a sharp ray caught on a shard of glass.

Madness, alone, awake.

BENNET SEARCHED for contusions and blood in her scalp and found none. Her phone was gone. Her backpack emptied and crushed. Clothes torn, body bruised, back sore, and a hip that cried out against bearing weight, Bennet wanted to scream and shove Peter away. He was infected and insane. But she needed to get to safety. She needed a crutch.

Convincing him to help her hike out of the woods seemed too easy after his erratic confession. She worried she was playing into some delusional trap. It was impossible to tell. Everything about Peter was unpredictable now. Bennet tried to place when the change in him had begun. What had she missed? Searching her memories led her down fond paths fraught with strange trepidation. Happy intimacies read as warnings in retrospect. Perhaps the sign like a seed had lain dormant in him all along.

They lurched together through forest brush. Her eyes drifted shut.

Peter caught Bennet mid-fall. "Whoa, let's stop here."

"No, I'm fine."

"You need rest before battle."

"No, no. Keep on."

He eased her down on the woodland floor. The nook of a tree cradled Bennet's back. Moss and leaves cushioned her aggravated hip. It felt so good to stop moving and let the earth carry her weight. Fatigue felled her like a green sapling that bent to the forest floor.

"That's good, Adira. Get some sleep."

Peter's soothing whisper jolted her head up.

"Ugh, no. Getting dark."

"Here's the last of my water. Try to stay hydrated. I'll get a fire going before sunset." Peter tucked the emergency blanket under her arms, settled the canteen snug between her hands in her lap, and took off his backpack to nestle beside her as extra support for her swaying head. "Back in a bit. It's okay to rest."

He receded into the forest. The daylight grew dim.

"Hell," Bennet slurred. Her head slumped. The damn thing was too heavy. Overcome by slumber, it hung low like an overripe fruit.

Adira Bennet's head ripened and fell off. Sweet juices spattered on impact. The severed fruit rotted fast, offering a home to wasps, birds, and ants. Her skull softened as the skin husk became brown and mushy. It grew a fine fur of mold. Aging ammonia odors mingled with the musty undercurrent of gangrene in an abandoned pool.

Bennet saw green. The vegetation in the landscape didn't look right. Fallen branches on the forest floor shifted. Pale, rough-hewn limbs stained with dark sap appeared rounded, less angular than normal wood. Broken sticks stripped of bark jutted out of the ends. The sap was too red, the jutting parts too white. The thickness of the branches and texture of the bark was too creamy, too ginger-toned, too softly modelled. Some sort of manikin, disassembled. No, that wasn't quite it. The limbs were too bloody, tumescent from abuse. Limbs. The branches were body parts.

They were her body parts. She felt the agony of their recent torture, recognized the sensations as hers. The realization of her impossible state pounded Bennet's severed head with pain. Pain drilled a tunnel through her brain. Pain popped her joints and ground them out of the sockets where her bones had been snapped.

Her butchered torso opened like a book. Rib fingers spread the wound open from within and displayed an unnatural split. The green on the forest floor was mildew covering broken tile, algae blooming on an abandoned pool. The humid expanse was bordered by cracked windows, absent panes, and garbage that sparkled with shattered glass.

Speedy decay enveloped her violated, scattered limbs. Her pungent head attracted a predator to feed. Bennet panicked with no way to fight as the rhythmic threat of an animal attack panted at the frayed base of her skull.

The black dog circled the bruised fruit of her head. Trotting in a wider circumference, it licked a stain below a tawny forearm that lay bent like a tender branch. The dog sniffed the end and lapped at the bone and trailing ligaments. It swallowed the limb down in one smooth gulp.

Sniffing the next nearby part, a human foot, her foot, no mistaking it for anything else, no logic to explain it but she knew, she could feel the agonizing pulse in her ankle, the vicious motion of the cut. The black dog grew larger. It tested her meat. It made another quick meal, growing and growing with each subsequent part. The dog devoured Adira Bennet's limbs until its vast jaw opened wide enough to fit her split torso. Devil-faced and ravenous, the animal forced her forked trunk down its guzzling throat.

More than five feet long, the dog had attained prehistoric canid dimensions. It moved with hefty shoulders and listened with large pointed ears. The massive round head housed a strong, flat maw. Black lips slanted across its razor teeth. Thick, the long tongue lolled at Bennet's head. It was the last portion of her left. Carrion breath huffed, bringing water to her dry eyes. She squeezed them shut. The tongue scraped the lids back up and salivated on her deflated face.

Her head rocked. The verdant gore that spread across her field of vision nodded yes. Adira Bennet's pain subsided as cavernous jaws closed over the last swollen, fallen fruit.

The dog-like Epicyon made a round of the pool perimeter before it leapt.

INTO THE DEEP END, algae laden water swirled in a green funnel where she splashed. An underwater summit opened to a vast expanse of seawater. The prehistoric canid threaded her way through submerged caves and plunged over the blind edge. Dense webs of stars strung through the black salty depths, lighting the Epicyon's natural habitat. She swam through oceans of time and tracked ancient paths, a dimensional traveler unbound by need for an external craft.

By serpentine tributaries, by powerful paws and muscular haunches, she came upon a spot where the water temperature warmed. Sensing her destination, she swam up. A red glow suffused the water. She broke the surface.

The lake was red. The shore was yellow. Ochre dunes elevated the terrain as far as her eyesight spanned. Dead things lay under the drifts, some centuries old, some fresh. The smell of delicious carrion called her, foul and sickly sweet. The Epicyon's belly ached with its burden of Adira even as she salivated at the promise of a feast.

Copious red water streamed from her black shape as she climbed out of the lake.

Ruins of immense towers crumbled on the bleak horizon. The Epicyon loped toward distant remains perched on a tall, forbidding dune. The twin black suns of Carcosa sank lower over the ruin. Black shadow fingers splayed like squid ink across mountains of yellow sand. Like smoky cracks, the shadows of sunset fractured the diseased land. The canid shook her coat dry. Red water pock-marked the yellow dune. Faces of plague spattered in the sand. Climbing over a crowd of sick leers, pushing against swirling blasts of wind, the Epicyon's deep paw prints crushed the clamoring faces. Lost souls screamed in the wind. Flying grit erased each step as she passed.

Inhabitants of Carcosa, crazed carrion crying for death, broken temples like bodies, land built of their ruin, flesh crumbled to sand. Grains of consciousness crying, wind howling for a sacrifice. The Epicyon's cargo a kingdom inverted.

The angry meat in her belly incubated. She carried all she'd swallowed between the beginning and end of time, between the mirrored bookend doors of history. Her internal metabolic process differed from biological digestion. It was an act of love, similar to the metamorphosis taking place inside the semi-mechanical, semi-organic, semi-sentient chrysalis that connected through multiple planes of existence, the incomprehensible weapon that now hatched in an underground military bunker lab.

METAMORPHOSIS WAS IMMINENT.

In the laboratory bunker, beneath the undulating foothills, inside the monstrous mask of the engineered insect chrysalis, the experimental weapon organized its contents and became whole.

Hybridized from biometric compounds, from insect and human proteins, powered by carbon-based nanomachines, the weapon's armor of neural tissue matured like a sudden missile strike. The chrysalis glowed. The shell thinned and became transparent. The weapon woke up.

Intrinsic to its design, to every cell that sensed information and stored concomitant memories, consciousness arose in the final stage of development. Previous instars had pulsed with neural threads, the organism a community of sentient impulses, the body a collaborative dream of multitudes. Their collective behavior worked by blind hive instinct, feeding, dreaming, and growing. Now a coherent totality aggregated inside the chrysalis. Woven of many eyes and many minds, the weapon's neural tendrils spread across invisible dimensions. The core contained an idea of identity, of will.

Professor Peter Krause had brilliantly designed the self-actualizing weapon to spin a storyline inside its shell based on prompts programmed and plagiarized from his lover's pseudo-history, a book he should not have read. The weapon called itself Adira. It knew what Bennet knew. It understood the battle it was invented to fight. It remembered the project's previous failed weapons, detected the numinous nature of its enemy, and experienced Peter's pressure on Director Bennet to be its pilot.

The weapon strongly agreed with Bennet that this was a bad idea.

After calculating probable outcomes for an infinite number of scenarios, a sociologically, emotionally, and mathematically masterful feat accomplished in mere seconds, the weapon decided to pilot itself.

Adira knew itself as a thing born of chaos, a body of dreaming neural impulses capable of defeating hallucinations that no gun, bomb, or army could target. She simultaneously embraced her mission to conquer the Yellow Queen, and accepted Peter's faith that she embodied the Yellow Queen. All possibilities merited equal consideration. Her programming compelled her to close the gap through which an imaginary and altogether unlikely galaxy leaked its madness-inducing poison into the human world.

Madness dwelled in her DNA, passed down from her mother. As the heir of the Queen in Yellow, the weapon was a thing of madness. She inhabited the enlightened, unbalanced, invisible sphere where smaller minds broke down.

Pleasurable chemical signatures contrasted within her chrysalis. Paradox equaled orgasm. In the personal primordial soup of her shell, Adira spun and swirled, generating futures and histories. Three legs spiraled out from the pivotal key at the center of the symbol in her spine. The Yellow Sign's spokes grew identities on a perpetually spinning wheel. Real or imaginary, no single story held true in isolation. The weapon amused itself with the thought that its own creation story was unreal, and for a moment like a millennium, it winked out of existence.

A WOOD FIRE BURNED, perfuming the autumn chill. Sadness, comfort, and hope wafted on the nostalgic smell of smoke. Cold air scented by the crisp tang of leaves that cascaded and corroded into dust, feeding the soil, nurturing the smallest terrestrial lives, microbial lives perpetuating an essential, invisible community that held the planet's ecosystem intact. A tattered canopy of yellow leaves drifted down in dusk.

A barren tree supported her back. Strange dreams entangled with the fond aroma of a campfire woke her up. A melody called Bennet's eyelids to open, her consciousness to come back from its noetic journeys. Peter's clear tenor travelled on the chilly air that divided Bennet's warm body from the cold echo of his song:

My lost heart bled beneath the sands
Of distant, dead Carcosa.
My heart, once buried, fed the land
That grew the oak Carcosa.

The oak was felled and burned to light
Those dim shores of Carcosa.
Love's but a candle. Soon I'll die
To wander lost Carcosa.

My love's a dream, and dreams must die
To resurrect Carcosa.
My dream is dead. My queen's alive.
She conquers bright Carcosa.

And she opened her eyes wide. And Peter looked down at her from a strangely constructed pyre. Bennet's head fell back on the tree trunk. Peter stopped singing. Worms of sweat twined with beads of tears furrowing down the crevices of his contorted face.

"All for you, my new Queen."

The smell of scorched rubber undermined the autumn calm of kindling. Flames teased the heavy soles of Peter's hiking boots. White smoke sent a stench of pollution down the canyon's deep cleft.

Inside a rough cage, bound by knotted sticks, Peter shuddered atop an infant blaze.

His hands were free. He was strong enough to break the flimsy trap. Unless it was not a cage to hold him in, but a barrier, more incantatory than material, against something he feared from outside.

Peter shrieked as a tongue of fire grew long and licked his leg. Bennet caught the whiff of burning hair and bolted upright. Peter's face creased in a grotesque mask of fanatic screams. "For you, all for you." Smoke encircled him like spider's silk. The voice cocooned within choked and cracked. "My life for you. My queen, ordained: my Queen in Yellow."

IV. IMAGO: TERRIBLE HANDS

Twin black suns sank in the lake of Hali beneath dim Carcosa, orbs exaggerated in size by the flesh of the woman's face receding into a mask of bone. Eyes aglow with darkness, love so strong it looked like hate. She would teach Adira strength. It was better to let her body wither and rot than become an object of pity and medical interventions. No doctor's indifferent hands should be allowed to peel away her hard-won pride.

The mobile home in need of repairs kept spotlessly clean. Her posture unbent by poverty. Never rich, but the women of her family displayed a certain poise and elegance. Beauty passed down through generations wasted on Adira, who rejected ease and happiness.

She buffed the polish in small swirls, attentive to the decorative silver hands. The pink, milky fluid formed a paste that stuck in every crevice. The intricacy of the carved clockwork prosthetics made the hands difficult to clean. Black tarnish nested in the tiny grooves of the mechanical masterpieces, too precious for her feckless daughter's possession. Adira's mother squeezed flesh-colored polish from a plastic bottle and rubbed with scraps of old t-shirts. She shined the silver hands until they were perfect, and locked them inside the curio cabinet.

She sighed. Everything with Adira was hard. Where did she go wrong? Her face smudged with pink paste, black residue, and hollow tears.

In the mirror, the lake, the lesson of symmetry was silenced. On the surface of the mask, the impasse of the unseen side's silvering swallowed a kingdom of stars. "I have done my best," she stated to the mirror, backbone rigid, chin held high. After cleansing, she moisturized with expert strokes, careful not to stretch the delicate skin underneath her eyes.

Nothingness reflected in the lake. The absence of stars spoke, spreading the sickness she felt in her marrow, the sickness that strangled her second child before it was born. Left her alone with a changeling, a challenge, a mirror of loss. A mask of truth.

I know your weakness. I know your flaw. I know your hidden monster spot. I know the tattered flags of pleasure you fly on raw winds, the yellow tatters you strip from your flesh to silence your young. I know your secrets because I am your darkest secret.

I am the stain, the cancer, the truth you can never polish out.

LOST, lost, inarticulate, Adira dismembered and swallowed, lost in the bowels of the black Epicyon, riding inside the strong animal body. Her helpless scattered parts battered, flesh against flesh, dream against dream, as the prehistoric canid climbed up the dunes of lost Carcosa. With ascent, the air chilled. Inside the belly of the beast, Adira was warm. Hot intestines pressed her parts together, congealing her mass of hacked limbs.

Limb against limb, hot wounds bloodied by friction, burned by hate. Rage seeped from tattered ends of ligament and broken knobs of bone. Hot liquid rage seared the ends together and forged her joints anew. Blood, the milk of rage, cauterized her weeping holes and sealed off the warm center of her heart.

Heavy inside the Epicyon, Adira's flesh hardened and became whole.

BENNET FLEW at Peter's feet with the emergency blanket thrust forward like a shield. Pain vanished in adrenalin panic. She tackled and rolled with him, beating at smoke. The Mylar blanket flared. She kicked it away. It melted into a silver clot. The strange cage of branches Peter had built around his body cracked. Bennet bucked and elbowed, smothering any sign of flames. Peter fought against her. The interlocking web of broken sticks jabbed her gut, cut her arms, and reopened fresh wounds from their slide down the cliff.

Peter thrashed until coughing overcame his strength. Bennet curled away, aching in fear. Toxic air wafted away.

Dissipating smoke sauntered down the canyon in a black chemical trail. Peter's breath came shallow and fast behind Bennet's back. She dreaded what she'd see beneath the singed clothes covering Peter's legs.

His voice came out in a strangled grind. "I'll find another way to serve. All for you. My gift. My life for you."

"Don't put this on me. You need help."

Peter laughed, a morbid bubbling that turned Bennet's stomach. "She makes a mockery of my testament. Before the watchdog of Osiris, the sacred dance."

His words trailed off in a nauseating chuckle. Bennet turned over to face the damage. Her injuries pounded in protest. Peter remained on his back wheezing, spitting swift words between stolen breaths. "The spirit is willing, the flesh is willing, neither is weak. Immortality is ours. Your kingdom is within me, copulating vipers, a stone, a tree, less noble, illusions of war."

Peter's breath faded. His dingy pallor from weeks underground exsanguinated further. The sweat on his forehead dried to paste. Foam clung to the corners of his cracked lips. Bennet forced her shoulders up, bones ringing with echoes of trauma.

She meant to check his airway, but first she had to throw up.

Flowers peppered her vomit. Bennet smelled them in full bloom. Cloying perfume of dew trembled in large globules of sap, petals licking at her mask that hung heavy and pallid over the substance she'd expelled. Bennet hissed at the stab of stomach cramps. Her saliva dropped on the flowers. The blooms curled like lips and slurped the sap. Bennet shrank into an insect perched on a monstrous tongue. Her sight focused into a funnel that ended in the pinpoint of a carnivorous throat.

Bennet shuddered and willed her eyes open. She hauled her face back from the garish colors of the bouquet erupting out of her vomit and shivered again. She realized she was cold. She felt Peter's forehead with her wrist. He was colder. She searched for a vein pulsing in his neck and found a weak yet consistent beat buried under his skin.

She thought he might be in shock. Given his outbursts, maybe it was for the best. Or was shock dangerous, even deadly? She reached for her phone and then remembered it was gone. Checking Peter's pockets, Bennet found only a keycard and nutrition bar. His skin felt cold and he remained still as she rifled through his vest. Too still, too cold. She took off her jacket, wrapped him tight, and rubbed the surface. Peter muttered strange, half-formed words. She rubbed harder. Although Bennet didn't understand what he said, she took any response as a good sign.

"That's it. Stay with me."

The team and military controllers at the lab knew they'd gone on hiatus for a day hike. She was the program director and he was the lead cognitive neuroscientist. As essential personnel, their prolonged absence would be an emergency. All Bennet had to do was keep Peter stable for a few more hours, maybe another day.

But hadn't it already been two days since the fall? It seemed the sun was always setting when she paid attention to the time. It was setting again now. She'd been in and out of sleep since he hurled them down the canyon. If his fit had sent them over a steeper cliff, they'd both be dead now. Bennet couldn't reconcile the image of her trusted lover with the man who tried to murder her any more than she could reconcile the unnatural merging and rewinding of time on the mountain.

She recalled visions of two sunsets interspersed with strange dreams. Was this the third sunset? Or had her dreams altered her perception of the passage of time? Perhaps one slow, lingering sunset seemed like many between the flashcards of disturbing dreams. Her last one —an endless torture dream of her body hacked apart and devoured by a mythical beast—may have lasted in real-time for mere seconds. With no phone to check, with her inner turmoil triggered by Peter's emotional collapse, Bennet chose to align with the simple, logical explanation. She was injured. She'd had restless sleep.

Because it didn't matter if the same sun still set, or if an imposter took its place. It didn't matter because Bennet and Peter faced dehydration or infection if someone didn't search for them soon. Bennet checked Peter's throat. His tongue wasn't swollen. He breathed. What next? Some sort of bandages? She peeled the charred wool socks down his calves with squeamish hesitation. Was it the right thing to do? They came off clean and revealed angry red skin. Above the socks, his shins blistered. But no yellow fire-eaten flesh, no cavities of bone. Bennet poured the last of the water over his wounds to clean them.

Peter didn't mumble or flinch. She checked for his pulse and found it again. Breathed again.

The nylon smell of his boot mesh burning had roused

Bennet from sleep. She unlaced the mauled shoes that had saved his life and pulled his socks off the rest of the way. "You'd make a lousy inquisitor. If you read outside your field more, you'd know they burned witches barefoot." She tossed the acrid, stinking items off in the direction of the dead fire. "Lucky for you, you always ignore me when I tell you to explore new interests. I suppose you'll never let me forget about this."

Half expecting Peter's amused protest, she paused.

Bit her lip, denied the surge of hot tears.

Maybe this was how it started. Bennet choked down a hopeless chill that rose in her throat. This was how cities emptied out and the world went feral. One person acted in sickness, and then a couple, a family, a scout group or ball club out at the park blinked off the map, lost in an instant. Lost in the wild, wounded, isolated. Coerced into the cult of the Yellow Sign, unwilling renegades seized the spurious marker of power in their struggle to survive. Logic and reason deteriorated through a new natural selection process spurred by fear, rumor, and mass hysteria. Humanity descended into something much worse than animals.

The human brain in its most regressive state retained powerful cognitive capacity and exploitable neurons ripe for the interventions of a perverted rewiring. Reports from endemic areas of infection outside of abandoned cities such as Houston and Slidell showed a spiral into primal violence more mindless than self-cannibalism, more deliberate than the Dionysian sacrifice at the brutal heart of Greek tragedy. Animal and tribal models failed to describe the horror of the new monstrous human. The rites of the Yellow Sign demanded a performance of inversion, a strangled twin held upside down above a crematorium's relentless fire.

The language of the cult was the sound of the sacrificial infant's screams. Its code remained disorganized, the hypnotic sigil an incomprehensible glyph despite persistent, oblique, unconscious influence. No species on earth behaved in such a disordered way, practicing gleeful self-annihilation coupled with obscene environmental savagery. Scant evidence survived of the atrocities. Vestiges of troops and field investigators returned. The majority defected to the horde. Unfortunates, innocents, soldiers, and priests were lost to the wild, as if humankind had lived too long in self-domesticated, communal captivity and craved a cosmic fate. The new primal human exploded both modern culture and ancient sacrificial myth. Blasting away the last shabby remnants of the comfortable cage, they worshiped something darker, less human, less animal. Less earthly.

The Yellow Sign spun its web with pestilent clarity, a sickle slashing reason, the breath-wheel of the dragon, new dharma of destruction. A king unsacrificed. A coronation ceremony in reverse. Images of the spray-painted symbol she'd seen in the photographs of rubble reminded Bennet of an unsettling memory she couldn't quite place. The significance of the sigil nagged at the edges of her awareness. Once seen, the Yellow Sign haunted a multitude of other shapes. She seemed to see it everywhere: in the tropism of bare branches, in the ash that smeared her skin, and in the web of veins that cracked Peter's sealed eyelids with blue fissures of light.

Averting her eyes, Bennet focused on the practical task of tending the worst burns on Peter's calves. With the remains of a first aid kit, she squeezed antiseptic ointment on a poncho, shredding it into strips, and wrapping his burns. The tube of ointment was tiny. Bennet tore it open with her teeth and peeled it apart to get the dregs. No question there wasn't going to be enough.

Peter remained immobile.

The slippery sides of the small tube defied her prosthetic grip. She fumbled, and the ointment dropped in the dirt, wasting what little was left.

"Helpless, fucking helpless!"

Her mind was a black spiral of rage. The insistent omen of the Yellow Sign bloomed in fertile, blind emotion, a demonic seedling sprouting in dark soil.

She remembered the book. Like a wounded three-legged spider, the sign crawled up the spine. The book was displayed on the hutch of her mother's curio cabinet, along with other books artfully arranged for show. Adira Bennet had never seen her mother sit down and read. The garish yellow spine, the squirming black creature where the title should be: conundrums such as these riddled Adira's childhood with dread. The mobile home was small. Her mother's massive antique took up one wall of the den. Adira had no shelter from the sight of the haunted, repulsive book.

The cloying yellow color caught her eye from the kitchen. The spinning black spider greeted her when she walked through the front door. It was the last thing that blighted her eyes when she left for school and the first thing that reached for her with dirty black fingers when she returned. If she watched TV, the book spied her from the hutch, eyeing her side. Wounded legs of a spider straggled black against yellow glare. Though Adira turned away, the putrid fluorescent glow competed with the screen.

At age eight, Adira's chores upgraded to include dusting. Scared of contact with the book, she wiped around the edges of the shelf for three weeks until her mother discovered the film of accumulated dirt. She slapped Adira's face.

"Those were your grandmother's books. Show some respect. Don't you care about anything?"

Bravely then, at first with rubber cleaning gloves on, she forced her fingertips to graze the slim edge of the spine, poked and slid the book around the shelf as she cleaned. Habituation reduced the threat of poison. She picked it up and replaced it fast. Brevity minimized contamination. Adira never opened the yellow book, never risked a glimpse of the contents until her mother lay dying.

It was an accident. Her mother languished, unconscious, much as Peter did now. Dutiful teenage Adira, helpless to change the course of the dragon's decline, incensed by the gloating symbol, gloating like an emblem of her mother's power while spinning that power and life force away through the vortex of its malicious presence; Adira grabbed the damned thing off the shelf, stomped outside to the end of the lot, and threw it in the dumpster.

Rage made her a bad shot. The book hit the side of the rusty bin. It landed open and face up. The pages spread for her. They were blank. Adira came closer and flipped a page with a reluctant shove of her foot. Nothing. With curious but careful prosthetic fingers, she raised it from the dirt and scanned the volume all the way through.

The book was an unwritten, antique journal. The pages were yellow with time.

Adira laughed. Her greatest fear was nothing, nothing at all.

Adopting the unused journal as her favorite notebook, making a pet of the malevolent monster that haunted her childhood, Adira worked on her math homework by her mother's bedside. In silence, always listening for the reassuring rasp of the next breath, the consistency and rationality of calculations gave comfort under the hovering pall of death. The embossed black spiral on the yellow cover and slender spine had a pleasing smoothness to its raised tendrils. The illusion of dread utterly slipped away. Adira's prosthetic fingers toyed with the texture of the bulging symbol, its contrast with the flat, worn swath of tattered linen wrapping the cover, and the vague but clean floral, vanilla, and paste scented spread of un-inked pages. She worked through complex formulas while she attended the dragon-mother skull-mother's bedside and listened for the slightest change in the sleeping woman's breath.

There was no story in the journal. Peter's claim of theft was evidence of his delusion. Now that Bennet recognized the Yellow Sign, she assumed many similar journals must have been manufactured, thus explaining the symbol's omnipresence. The three-legged spiral must have been a common antique publisher's mark. That she'd never noticed it before the outbreak was simple inattention. Once the cult seized upon it, the Yellow Sign, like a self-fulfilling prophecy, appeared ubiquitous.

Her tears fell on Peter's face. His sallow skin absorbed them like a blank page turned yellow with time. Frustration and grief blurred her past and present. She took a deep breath and focused on the current threat.

Peter shouldn't have easy access to a blunt object. She lugged broken branches out of his immediate reach. Using a large stable limb as a crutch, she hobbled a short distance away and hid behind a clump of dense brush. The crutch doubled as a weapon if Peter woke up.

When he wakes up, she corrected, daring to hope.

Bennet felt used up, like leftover a husk. Panic had lent her strength. Symbiotic fear had fed on her body while feeding it, and now her extreme fatigue seemed a more numinous exchange of energy than the predictable chemical crash of spent adrenalin. As Bennet's eyes fluttered shut, a swarm of butterflies landed, puddled, and fed upon her flowery vomit.

THE YELLOW QUEEN pressed her face into her fists. Raw sockets in her skull ground against the fleshless fingers of her hands. Bone against bone, gap against gap, she scored her sockets deeper until her vision went black. Dry tears strangled in her exposed throat.

Nothingness craved expression through the conduit of her bones. She strived to contain a disordered cosmology in her heavenly body. The royal design of an organized universe positioned the celestial sun as the king, the moon as the queen, and the stars and planets as attendants and courtiers. The sun gave off light and the moon reflected it.

But what of a king who gave off darkness?

What inversion did she reflect? By mirroring an inversion, did the doubly reversed image achieve transposed form? Or was Hastur forever and forever formless? Was the queen's body a universe, or a signifier of universal opposites?

Moon madness glowed in the mirror of her eyes. The vacuums of her empty sockets filled with charged particles like optical devices machined in a modern silvering process. They eliminated distortion by switching the reflective surface to the front of the glass. In ancient monarchies, as in chess, the king stood behind the reflection. He was the black coating on polished metal, an existence implied by absence. He dwelled in the devices and detritus of outdated technology, yellowing like the blank pages of unwritten books. His obsolete darkness undermined the Yellow Queen's comprehension of light.

Bitterness welled up from the maelstrom of nothingness in the cavity of her chest. Aching bone, alone, alone, with pain her consort and guide, her skeletal frame shook as black madness billowed from inside. She was a good mother. She hid her skeleton beneath her garments, kept her yellow tatters cleaned and pressed, and wrapped the rags as tight as false ligaments. Flesh-mummy, her hips were slender, her shoulders tall, her cheekbones well-sculpted. Her hair was a yellow crown. A harmless human exterior hid the hunger within.

Adira's mother gave birth to madness. She knew no

king, knew only empty tears, and swallowed the seeds of betrayal sown by imposters. They sank through her bones, dripped between her legs, and cooled like wax into the putrescent yellow labia that oozed from her stabilizing wraps. Hungry tentacles distended, curled, and craved. They salivated for the satisfaction of submissive flesh. A piece of flesh to pad the pain of her emptiness, to cure the endless aching of her exposed bones.

The soft, delectable flesh of an infant to hold.

ACROSS LICHEN and scrub grasses frozen in verdant dormancy, Adira's arms and legs swelled within the pelt. Slick and black as a panther, loping free and jubilant as a dog, Adira's reorganized substance filled the Epicyon's skin. Lithe muscles responded to her impulses. Rock and bramble toughened the charcoal-colored pads on her paws. The enormous nine-foot canid shook its pointed hyena ears and huffed from large, rounded jaws. When Adira breathed through its wide nostrils, cool wind howled into her new lungs.

Snow had replaced the yellow sands immeasurable miles below. Black silhouette on a white peak, Adira the animal lapped at ice to quench her thirst. She dug the hidden crocus bulbs that nourished her powerful form. She inhaled the night air of Carcosa like a drug. Her new body was as black as the inverted stars that sank in the lake of Hali.

Director Bennet dreamed the same sleek blackness and celestial expanse in the forest mountain gulch. Her injured, unconscious body dreamed a multitude of heavenly bodies beneath the animal's black curtain of flesh. Sounds quelled. Nothing reflected in the still surface of the lake. Nothing rippled or whispered from its noiseless plane. On the other side of the mirror, the lake's message of symmetry was denied in the smooth indifference of its silvering.

Engaged, intent, and ecstatically far from indifferent, the weapon ceased her playful permutations in and out of various dimensions and chose a state of existence familiar to her zookeepers, as she'd named the team in the bunker. Her habitat sensors instantaneously fried. Alerts went off. A lab tech rushed in. The young man had serious glasses and disorderly hair. The weapon enjoyed his serious and diligent distress. He tweaked buttons and shook his head at the readouts, checking the monitor again and again. Then he frowned over the console and peered into her cage.

She hatched.

The cocoon split. A woman dropped out. She was slimy and naked. She landed on her feet with an agile forward lunge and walked through the heavy-duty wall of the enclosure as if the triple-layered acrylic sheet was a curtain of air.

The tech stumbled back against the console behind him. The weapon came forward and circled his shaking wrists. With precise fingers, she pulled his hands to her belly and slid them down into the viscous and plentiful slime between her thighs. The tech trembled and didn't seem to be able to breathe correctly. She observed him with more interest than concern. Pressing his palms together, she slid them inside and wrenched up to her heart, splitting her torso in half.

The weapon swallowed the tech with the lips of her torso. He squirmed as she closed around him. He had no time to argue or react. Her digestive juices flowed. His thoughts melted. She knew everything about him. Communion felt nice.

Really, really nice.

His agonized writhing reminded the weapon she was supposed to be the hero. She spit out the lab tech alive and unfurled her wings. Below her expanding, monstrous form, the man shook off her copiously streaming secretions, prattled about god and demons, and stared up at her numerous spawning fingers like exponential owl feathers that spanned twenty feet wide and blacked out the fluorescent ceiling fixtures. The glow of fire in her veins suffused the lab with deep red light.

Behind the radiant nude figure that the tech would later describe as a flaming liquid angel of death, her proliferating digits beat like proud predator feathers and merged into a giant pair of hands. They opened wide and alternately clenched into fists. She paused, palms up, to thank the man. He was a satisfactory brain snack. Then she wrapped her molten body with her wings, threaded her giant fingers together in thought, and spun fast enough to ignite. She burned and guttered out of sight.

THE EPICYON RAN free of her reflection. She roared and leaped high over ragged peaks. Snow turned ochre in false sunlight. Atop the tallest summit, a grotesque throne of beeswax and gossamer secretions glinted with poison liquids that dripped like golden tar. The throne emitted a venomous light. The ground for miles below was heaped with bare branches, bleached like a field of bones. Pallid mounds of amputated limbs reflected the yellow hue of the glowing throne in a mirage, a lie of sunrise.

Something twisted in the sky.

Black on black, the three uneven tendrils of the Yellow Sign rotated on a fleshless axis. The Epicyon lunged into the bowels of the baroque exudate beneath the throne. Her paws grew sticky with poison. Threads like spun glass cut her pelt as they broke away, gold strands splashing in wax. If she slowed, she sank in amber sludge. The beast leaped, licked her paws, and burst through to the cramped den of the derelict mobile home.

Adira's mother turned after locking the silver prosthetics inside the curio cabinet. "Oh, dear. What have you done now?"

The Epicyon planted her front paws on the curio cabinet and pinned the frail woman underneath. The scarred pelt parted like black curtains to reveal daughters of different ages on an opulent stage. The rich red hue of innards formed a canopy above the ivory dais of bone where Adira and Bennet met wearing their respective masks. Their mother loomed in the glass doors of the curio cabinet, growing larger, more mummified, then more skeletal, her grinning skull crowned by a flayed blond scalp. The silver hands behind the glass mangled her reflection further, spinning her limbs into a three-legged wounded spider as she strained to reach the stage.

The Yellow Sign spiraled to life. The reflection took form. A wheel of gold fire melted the silver hands in the curio cabinet. Molten metal pooled on the floor. Heat seared and rippled around its circumference. Where the metal burned, the floor fell away and created a chasm. The pool dropped and spread across the bottom. The glass doors melted, and the wood scattered to ash. Liquid glass spread atop the silver pool. The fluids cooled into a mirrored lake immeasurable miles below.

The spinning sign slowed. The flat reflection darkened into a solid three-dimensional form. Three black points like inverted stars studded an astronomical diadem. The sharp edges of the weapon's coiled crown spun and slashed the Epicyon's throat. The blood of the animal erased the stage and washed away the masks. The Yellow Queen seized the actors in the cages of her bony fingers. After the red deluge ceased, the fallen black curtains of animal flesh unveiled an alien sky above her. A towering structure reared over the frozen peaks of lost Carcosa.

The throne erupted in secretions from the skeletal body of Adira's mother. The Yellow Queen dangled her captured daughters over the abyss of the chasm. Three forms doubled below in the distant mirrored lake.

The Yellow Sign as diadem doubled as a spinning star and weapon. The tendrils of the weapon slowed their manic slashing and softened into sympathetic fingers. Circular, the crown split into symmetrical halves. Fingers like feathers shaped into the wings of an owl. Wings bulked into the fleshy span of a pair of giant hands that spread from the weapon's shoulders. In humanoid form, with her fire contained safe in her veins, the weapon met the iridescent glow at the apex of the poison throne.

The weapon encircled Adira, her mother, and Bennet in the cyclone of her firm wings. For a moment, the unstable spinning of the three-limbed Yellow Sign ceased. Child, woman, weapon, and queen all balanced in a shared orbit. An underlying dance of chaos sustained the balance of the visible world.

Beside her mother's sickbed, Adira rubbed the raised imprint on the cover of the yellow book with a fascinated finger. The embossed texture called to her like a scar. A subtle sensation of pleasurable disturbance transmitted from pen to prosthetic to the practiced nerves in Adira's arm. The asymmetrical spiral of appendages suggested less a mystery and more a set of keys.

College was too easy, the joy of defiance too brief while facing death. As her mother slept, Adira curled with the journal in a sunken armchair by the bed and contemplated what path or portal the sigil unlocked. Accounting for the speed and trajectory of its implicit motion, she experimented with balancing the unstable design in the language of equations. Her calculations described the spatiotemporal patterns of the Yellow Sign, its deviations and potential values. Adira was at the top of her class, yet the solution eluded her or the theorem was false. The math didn't work. Perhaps when she learned more advanced calculus, she might express the complex truth obscured by a deceptive appearance of simplicity in the sickly symbol.

Obsession replaced anxiety. The math called to her like a scar. Adira declared her major. As her mother lay dying, the pages of the antique journal grew sticky, inked with her intricate webs of math.

Once terrible and commanding, the dragon now rarely stirred. Adira honored her mother's wishes to eschew hospice. Bathing, feeding, and toileting were external acts of love easily done without the hindrance of true emotion. After all, Adira had years of experience performing on her mother's cardboard and papier-mâché stage. Unable to satisfy the dragon's lust for a proper sacrificial starlet, Adira mapped perfection in the structural beauty and reason of mathematics. She knew she had the ability. She just needed more education, more time. More light as the dragon's fire faded. Adira endured constant criticisms and insults from the sick woman in exchange for a delay of her final silence.

The song of the dying dragon waned. The enfeebled wheeze pervaded every nook of the cramped home. Adira drifted to sleep on the lingering, intermittent rasp and woke in terror to make sure it was still there. It was the last thing she listened for when she hesitated before she left for class, and the first thing she checked on when she braved its absence and came back in through the door.

One night, as Adira wrestled to balance the resistant equation of the trickster sigil, she noticed after a long interval of quiet that she herself had stopped breathing. A black sensation of airlessness clutched at her throat. Desperate pain compressed her chest and begged her to nourish her lungs. Her cells screamed for air. Her rib cage convulsed. Her tongue pulsed on the roof of her mouth.

She inhaled. The sensation was like swallowing a fish whole. Scales and eyes and fins lodged where the hollow sound of the dragon's breath had long ago rattled and died.

Overwhelmed by silence, Adira sat beside the corpse. Uncertain how much time had passed, she stilled the hand that crushed the soundless, shared throat. She needed to breathe. She wrestled against its chokehold. The hand came free. Adira gasped, panted, and stared at the murderous thing.

It was not her hand. She'd lost both of hers in an episode of domestic violence. The mechanical appendages she wore served her well and functioned almost as accurately as natural ones, but no, these were not her real hands. She was not responsible for any of this. True, a mercy killing had taken place, and Adira was thankful for the release, thankful for her mother's suffering to finally end. The woman had become little more than a skeleton shifting in the tatters of her bed, saffron sheets worn threadbare, jaundiced skin stretched over bone. Adira had never before seen the angry jaw come unclenched, the glare gone blank, the dragon emptied, slack as a molted skin. She must call someone now that it was done.

Soon, soon, she would call soon. First, she must make sense of the paradox. Adira stayed with the body and buried her head in the folds of her mother's yellow-bound heirloom book, tracing the unsolved conundrum of the wounded three-legged spider: the spiral, the vortex, the sign. She wondered if the dead still dreamed, and if they did not, did it matter if she balanced the untenable equation. Despite the suspicion that it was now a useless task, it was not Adira Bennet's nature to give up. For several forlorn hours, she grappled with the math and what it might mean to be free.

Flowers in her hair, flowers in her eyes, flowers in her mouth. Crowned in her casket, the Yellow Queen dreamed with a possessive vengeance that tethered the girl to the grave-borne body, reached from unseen worlds to pull Adira through with hungry hands. Black stars shone above the yellow sands of Carcosa, peering across predatory time. Pummeling winds muted all sound, and Adira felt some strange cage interlock and lift her. Arms linked through her arms, leading her on the inverse trajectory of a bride up the aisle, away from the altar, through the mourners at the chapel doors, out to plod and sink in sodden cemetery grass. Multiple times and multiple forms intersected through Adira in the procession.

At the point of convergence, where greedy hands from the heavy casket claimed Bennet's prosthetics, claws of the dragon closed around her bleeding wrists. Old limbs fresh with new wounds, Bennet's arms wept streams of blood. Handless Adira knelt by the grave with her funerary bouquet, opened her mouth to say a final farewell prayer, and vomited bitter cyanide hydrangea down into the open hole.

Poison met poison, drooling strands of spit that seared

the dead flesh from the queen's craving bones. Above, weapon wings opened with the precision of an algebraic formula. The staring sockets of an empty pelvis split to span galaxies. A weightless abundance of owl feathers crushed reality into an inverted mass. Adira cried at the sight of her angel. Bennet cowered. She didn't recognize the thing she'd dismissed in late adolescence as a tortured hallucination.

The Yellow Queen bared her lipless teeth atop her grotesque throne in Carcosa and let her rags of pleasure fall away. Unwinding, unbinding, a mummified corpse unraveled her spiraling tatters to expose the vacuum around which she composed her bones. She was a body all bone, a skeleton seeking meat. A thing made of nothing, made of need.

Bennet gaped into the empty craters of skull, pelvis, and planet, black cavities where the queen pulled her prey inside. Desire both insatiable and unreasonable slathered back, a writhing mirror of mad love where Bennet sought the nurturance and calm of a still lake. Spewing tundra above and desert below, Carcosa nightmared into existence. The sickening height begged Bennet to plummet into the mirrored lake and crash or drown. With bleeding stumps, trapped by the claw of the monstrous skeleton atop her poison throne, Bennet knew madness and screamed.

The siren of her shriek awoke sleeping parts of her brain poised for battle.

Adira caught in the other claw reached out and took Bennet's hand.

Both of them had hands again. Hands of flesh and

blood, tools bestowed at birth, wise with responsive skin, warm with profound musculature. They threaded their hands together in wonder and held each other tight in one many fingered fist.

"Are you my sister?" Adira asked.

"No." Bennet admired the beautiful, passionate girl. She didn't know how to tell her she had so much strength, so much to learn. "Well, something like that. More of a friend."

Adira's gaze of adulation collapsed. She recovered and looked up with fierce camaraderie. "Close enough."

Hands determined and strong trembled against twin flesh. A cruel wind howled through empty bone, forlorn torment in a song of disordered sirens, muses of loathing and disgust. The skeleton of the Yellow Queen crackled like loose electricity.

Adira yelled over the storm: "Let me go. I killed her before. I can do it again."

Bennet held firm. Killing the dragon changed nothing. The queen was alive.

She had to pilot the weapon, whether she had the training or not.

The queen was alive. Two iliac crests loomed wide like a horned mask as the Yellow Queen pulled them toward the cavernous hole enclosed by her exposed pelvic bone.

Bennet tried to imagine the mature weapon in its final stage, to envision its movement or sound and call it forth to fight. She drew a blank, feeling she'd forgotten something essential, something on the edge of awareness. It was as if she woke from a dream overwhelmed with a sense of its significance, yet had no memory of the content. A storm of infinite rage blackened the air. Blue arcs sparked across white bone. The gap threatened to swallow her sanity as she circled inside the great skeletal beast.

This time Bennet didn't scream. An old wound of terror pierced her. She didn't flee into a mental safe place: she was going to die anyway, and the world along with her. Emptiness cored her from throat to groin. She didn't look into the void. She was the void.

The void had no limits, no end.

This was the battleground. This was the dream. Every moment she woke up. Every moment she forgot it was a dream and woke again. The weapon was in the gaps between the moments, between the conviction of waking and sleep, between the solid bones of the monstrous creature crushing her, and the horrific spaces that ogled, devoid of bone.

Bennet held Adira's hands. "It's us. We're the weapon."

"Let me go."

"The angel is the weapon. It's part of our story, our DNA. We can fly it."

"I'll kill all of you, everything. Let go of me!"

Adira raved. Bennet clasped her struggling hands. How she wished she had time to explain, to teach. She felt the same manic desire for revenge, the same thrill at possessing her lost limbs intact. She restrained the girl's desperate fists with mature, powerful hands, knowing she'd lose them again if they won the battle and ended the dream.

The pelvic mask loomed like a crazed face. Where the large bone jointed in the center, it split. Wings intersected in a complicated diadem and crowned the queen in a circle of flesh, an irrational angel, a multidimensional manifestation of the living Yellow Sign.

Constellations of black stars bloomed in the spiral shape. Individual pinpoints of absent light from imploded stars generated a new multitude of abysses. History unraveled with the peeling away of the queen's tattered rags. Astronomers encountered the Yellow Queen time and again through fissures in the universe. Her reflective surface suggested other deities, and she passed in and out of time unseen. Human reality grew frail and pockmarked with disease as her desire furrowed new channels of madness. Holes like the legacy of prions sentenced the cosmos to a state of puerile dementia. The Yellow Queen reproduced her own absence.

She needed lavish flesh, unctuous juices, the elasticity of immature meat. Meat caged like veal, fattened and immobilized for life. Not slaughtered, but slit open and tasted, stung into submission, slathered, bathed, and swaddled in lies. Her fingers of bone plucked at the fleshy diadem, the living sign circling her mother in a monstrous axis of unfulfilled desire.

With all her hands and wings and selves, the weapon embraced the Yellow Queen. Her tentacled web of arms made love to the spaces between the skeleton woman's bones. She deposited eggs, filling all the needy gaps. The eggs incubated and hatched. The larva of newborn weapons plumped up, maturing inside the protective cage of bone. Growing weapons re-meated the queen, hung pendulous from her skeleton, pupated in bulbous sacs, filled her cavities with writhing life. When metamorphosis was complete, the new weapons launched. Each dreaming neural body targeted a single pockmarked hole in the mad celestial sky.

Detonating in every abyss, they seeded healthy living tissue in the demented brain of the universe. A network of electrical impulses connected empty pockets of time. Myriad patterns of conscious thought awoke the pulses of dead stars. Revived, their fire splashed the sky with wild spectrums of light.

Below, the lake of Hali spread like a blind mirror. There was no reflection, not of sky or queen or weapon. As the unseeing mirror refused discourse, electrical light seared the black surface of the queen's angry eyes. Twin suns turned inward. The swirling motion of funnel clouds poured pigment into the skull and saturated the bones. They shook and fissured with violent color.

The skeleton woman faltered. Her brittle bones cracked. Entropy ground them to ash. Her skull flaked into sulfur dust. The exudate throne crumbled. Gold fragments crashed down. The remains were scattered on the howling thrusts of desert gales, leaving tattered monuments with unreadable epithets strewn across desolate sands.

Lost forever in Carcosa, the Yellow Queen reigned in the mute dunes and shifting body of the old astonished land.

CHOPPING, flickering, spinning; voices from above. A quick, shuddering vision of black tendrils shot through with light came cascading down. Downward, a complex woven trap clamped over her falling body. Bennet lashed out at what must be the venomous throne looming above as she plummeted through an endless black hole towards inescapable nothingness. Her prosthetic hands hit the branches of a twig shelter. Her thrashing head pulverized dead leaves. The fecund smell of leaf debris reminded her she was in the forest, in the canyon. No poison throne loomed, no eternal abyss swallowed her. She wasn't falling, only disoriented by the dizzy illusion of spinning.

Searchlights swept from above. A helicopter's black blades flickered and split the air. The canopy of branches filtered piercing beams of light.

Bennet was safe on the ground. The ache in her bruised hip proved the laws of the physical world applied. Time, space, and gravity were in order again.

Voices came near and then halted. Bennet heard shouts. A commotion several feet away, close to the remains of Peter's fire pit: *Oh, God,* she thought. She tried to turn, but her head was weighted with the queasy suspicion that Peter's madness had ended in death. The man that shoved her from a cliff and tried to burn himself alive was not the same man she loved and trusted mere days ago. Bennet didn't know how much of the violence came from Peter, how much from the sickness of the Yellow Sign. Regardless of its origin, if Peter was alive, she'd report his abuse without qualms.

She hesitated to look, aware some outraged part of her wished him dead. What if she still dwelled in a dreamscape where thoughts impacted reality? After twisting her neck in Peter's direction, Bennet kept her eyes closed and reasoned it through. Of course, she felt uncertain after what she'd experienced. It was miraculous she wasn't more mad than Peter. Even if she'd never trust him again, behavior born of brain damage didn't warrant a death sentence. She wished him alive. She opened her eyes. A cluster of activity cleared. Peter was bound to a stretcher. An oxygen mask covered his face.

Bennet exhaled. Not a body bag, a stretcher.

Sudden hands, not of bone or dragon claw or tentacled wing, but human hands deft and trained for emergency care lifted her on a count of three. Bennet recognized the uniforms with relief. She answered the medic's questions thankfully to prove her cognitive orientation: name, year, city, state.

"Good job, Director. How many fingers am I holding up?"

"Four."

"Okay, last one. What's three plus five minus eight?"

"Oh come on. Give me something harder."

"Answer the question. It's the last one we need you to do. What do you get when you solve the problem?"

"Zero."

"That's right. It's time to go home now."

The medic made a grim attempt at a smile. Bennet tried to ask about Peter's condition, but the medevac team worked too fast for her to interact. She relaxed as straps closed over her to assure safety on ascent. The grim little medic gestured to the helicopter pilot. Bennet's head and stomach lurched.

How strange to fly in a body without wings. The underbelly of the helicopter sprouted six legs and hummed with the friction song of a giant insect. In the cumbersome rescue contraption, Bennet's body swayed with corporeal weight. The pendulous motion was nothing like piloting the weapon, like communing with shared identities hovering on the cusp of enlightenment and madness, spanning timeless across galaxies, transcending history through intuitive flight.

Three plus five minus eight equaled zero, the same value as the absence of the equation. The medic with the grim smile demanded Bennet follow an inefficient route that circled back to the start, to arrive at nothing. The problem was nullified in its solution.

In sharing the drama of the weapon's dream, the diseased mind of the universe healed, and in healing, sealed off a safe space habitable for humans. Bennet didn't want credit for laying the Yellow Queen to rest any more than she wanted credit for creating monsters and angels to populate her childhood nightmares. She'd been a pawn in Peter's plan, entrapped by his strange faith. He required her to take on the mantle of usurping queen, as if Bennet had the power to weave together the tattered shreds of reality and don the thick raiment of the universe as her imperial cloak. If Peter knew her better, he'd have understood how heartily she shunned her mother's garments.

Poor deluded Peter. He employed the calculations in her adopted journal as if they represented a numerological code, not realizing the formulas were incomplete. He should have worked the math. One thing was clear and simple without checking the book. A queen made of absence, once destroyed, left no vacuum in her wake. The problem was nullified in its solution.

I'm no queen, Bennet thought, *and who says this world needs one? There is no absence. There is no need. The world is safe. I am enough.*

Rising in a wide, slow spin, lifted higher by the tow-lines, Bennet neared the churning rotors and the spiral emblem their motion mirrored on the belly of the chopper: the three-pronged Yellow Sign.

The common publisher's mark from Bennet's inherited journal was the same as the insignia on the breasts of the uniforms worn by the paramedics. It was engraved on the nickel serial-number plates bolted to the portable medical equipment. It was woven through the patterns of the thick poly-fabric straps that held Bennet in place, and it would mark the doors of the bunker, splitting in half when they wheeled her stretcher home. Splitting in half like a psychotic angel descending out of paradoxical time.

The Yellow Sign greeted Bennet from the helicopter underside. Blades endlessly cut, stilled by speed. The illusion of a circle comforted her. The weapon was within her; it was the angel, the sign made manifest, a part of Adira Bennet's sensory experience and neural network. It was everywhere she looked, an image floating in the liquid of her eye.

Solving the conundrum had been a personal puzzle, a game to focus her mind, a solace from the horror of her mother's death. She'd come close to completion of the correct formula in her first notebook. The pages of the antique yellow journal overflowed with notations and theorems. Equilibrium hovered there.

Hovering in the sky, falling into drowsiness despite the blast and bite of chopper blades, consciousness claimed by insistent sleep. What had once maddened Bennet about the sign called her home. A perfect answer waited for her, balanced on the threshold of awareness. She planned to pull the journal off the shelf, put the past behind her, and get to work solving the problem of the sigil for once and for all. How silly that she'd once feared it, once tried to throw the tome in the trash.

In her last waking moment between the blackness of sleep and the lucidity of dreaming, Adira Bennet's mind surged with the raw power of the sign. It wasn't good or evil. It held no poison or cure. The Yellow Sign transcended energy, like a dynamic sickle that slashed away preconceptions and paved the way for greater things. It slaughtered monsters and christened a new path with their blood. Holding out hope for a better future in its wake, Bennet saw with instant clarity how to correct her math.

ABOUT THE AUTHOR

Joe Koch writes literary horror and surrealist trash. Their books include *The Wingspan of Severed Hands, Convulsive,* and *The Couvade,* which received a Shirley Jackson Award nomination in 2019. His short fiction appears in publications such as *Vastarien, Southwest Review, PseudoPod, Children of the New Flesh, Brave New Weird,* and *The Queer Book of Saints.* Joe also co-edited the art horror anthology *Stories of the Eye* from WeirdpunkBooks. He/They. Find Joe online at horrorsong.blog and on Twitter @horrorsong.

ALSO BY JOE KOCH

Invaginies

The Shipwreck of Cerberus

Convulsive

The Couvade

ALSO BY WEIRDPUNK BOOKS

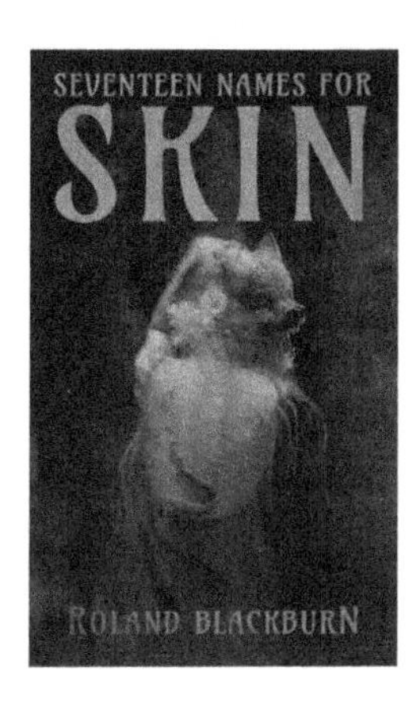

Seventeen Names for Skin by Roland Blackburn

After a cancer diagnosis gives her six-months to live, Snow Turner does what any introverted body-piercer might: hire a dark-web assassin and take out a massive life insurance policy to help her ailing father. But when a vicious attack leaves her all too alive and with a polymorphic curse, the bodies begin stacking up. As the insatiable hunger and violent changes threaten to consumer her, she learns that someone may still be trying to end her life. Can Snow keep her humanity intact, or will she tear everything she loves apart?

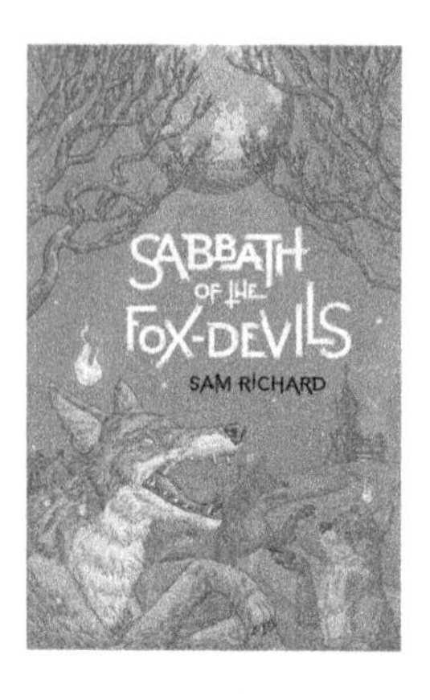

Sabbath of the Fox-Devils by Sam Richard

After learning about the existence of a powerful grimoire through a cartoon, 12-year-old Joe is determined to find it and change his lot in life. But in doing so, he'll also uncover a local priest's dark secret and how it may be connected to Joe's brother abruptly leaving town five years ago.

Part homage to the small-creature horror films of the 80s (*Ghoulies, Gremlins, The Gate*) and part Splatterpunk take on a Goosebumps book, *Sabbath of the Fox-Devils* is a weird, diabolical coming-of-age horror story of self-liberation in an oppressive religious environment set during the Satanic Panic. Prepare your soul to revel in the darkness.

"Light the black candles and invert the cross as Sam Richard conjures a coming-of-age story of Satanic panic, creature carnage, and blasphemous terror!"

— RYAN HARDING (*GENITAL GRINDER, HEADER 3*)

The Mud Ballad - Jo Quenell

NEVER BE ALONE AGAIN

In a dying railroad town, a conjoined twin wallows in purgatory for the murder of his brother. A disgraced surgeon goes to desperate ends to reconnect with his lost love. When redemption comes with a dash of black magic, the two enter a world of talking corpses, flesh-eating hogs, rude mimes, and ritualistic violence.

"Jo Quenell's debut novella explores both regret and connection in the weirdest and wildest ways possible. Good times!"

— DANGER SLATER (*IMPOSSIBLE JAMES, I WILL ROT WITHOUT YOU)*

Printed in the USA
CPSIA information can be obtained
at www.ICGtesting.com
JSHW021245260124
55892JS00001B/34